BASIC LOVE STORY

Episode 1:

The boy and the old man make friends

By

Ryan Austin Clarke

To: Christy
Your more beautiful than the
blonde who went to Church!
From: RA Clarke

ISBN: 0-75962-895-5

This book is printed on acid free paper.

1stBooks - rev. 07/23/01

TABLE OF CONTENTS

EPISODE I

The boy and the old man make friends.

Ryan Austin Clarke

CHAPTER 1

How to get your child out of bed in the morning.

Hi there! My name is John O'Reilly. That's Reilly with an Oh in the front. In fact, BIG 0 is what I have stamped on my personalized license plate attached to my antique motor vehicle valued at over four hundred thousand dollars. I make good money. The average personal income for the United States is $44,000, with the median at $23,000. In 2013 I did four times the average, $186,000. Not bad, considering in 1999 I was making $7 an hour. In 2014 I had a banner year. I raked in almost $600,000. 2015, last year, I hit a sour note and squeaked by with a little less than a $100,000. I don't know about this year. I do know I don't want to suck it up two years in a row. I have some potential business drawn up on the board for the month of December. I've got 30 days before the tallies done, and everyone counts their chips for the big dealer, the king of the hill, Uncle Sam.

But that's enough about money. Who am I kidding? When people want to get to know you, the first question they usually ask is what you do for a living. That way they can figure, from your profession, what your worth. Simply put, in a good year, by today's standards, I'm an outstanding heart surgeon. In a bad year, a family physician makes almost as much as I do. Speaking of families, I've got one of those.

My wife is a red hot blonde who knows how to shake her body. She only shakes it for me, not for you. In her forties, she frequently gets complements on not being a day over 35. Occasionally, she gets some gullible guy to believe she just looks old for 30. But not me, I know for a fact she is 43. Her age, 27, is on our marriage license. We were married in 2000 and I can do the math. Don't tell her I told you how old she is. She likes people to guess. It makes her feel good. A lot of women are that way. I stopped trying to guess why.

She's an animal doctor, properly referred to as a veterinarian. She lets the kids call her an animal doctor. I call her Dr. Doolittle when my little Princess is around. I've stopped calling her an animal doctor. The last time I did she retorted, "I don't know why a married a man like you!" So I responded, "Because you needed me to take care of you," to which she replied, "And you needed someone like me, an animal doctor, to fix you!" Like I said, she's a veterinarian.

I've had two offspring with my wife. I've got a 15 year old boy. I had the spring turned off after we had our second child, my little Princess. She was enough offspring for me. That kid's got a windup spring in her that never winds down. I've decided to keep the rest of that kid making stuff inside me where it belongs. Technically speaking, I've had a vasectomy. My wife likes to say my love pipe has been plugged. No, she didn't perform the operation, another woman doctor did. The fact next to nothing comes out has become a great equalizer. I can fake it almost as well as my wife does. She claims she knows when I do and when I don't. I know better.

I've never been happier in my life, until now. The computer just turned on the "wake up" music at 6am. The music has been carefully designed "to fully awaken one for the rigors of life." That's what I read on the package the music was boxed in. I should have suspected such a package with such a statement would contain anything but gentle music, but it gets me going. I slept four hours last night. Plenty for me. My wife sleeps more.

When I'm not in bed at 11pm and my wife wants some lovin', or sugar from big Daddy, namely me, she'll turn off Leno on TV, the bedroom lights, and leave our bedroom door wide open. But I have to show up before 12am, otherwise my Cinderella is out for the count. When my wife is exhausted, I can show up in the bedroom at 5am, to find all the lights on and the latest infomercial pitching some overpriced fad product on the boob tube. Lately, the TV has been selling "sex in a can." You spray it on your love stick and you turn into a bottle of unleashed sexual desire for only four easy payments of $89.95. That's what

4

the commercial said. Sometimes, if I'm lucky I can get "sex in a bed" at 5:50am with my wife. I have to rub on her for almost an hour before she wants some, and then she'll usually fake it for five minutes so she can get another five minutes of sleep. When you have kids sex when they're asleep is the only time you can get a "sex act in."

What Cinderella's carriage turned into, or what my wife made for me, Pumpkin, has an unpleasant habit of not getting up in the morning for another invigorating day of preschool. I don't blame my little Princess. She can do no wrong. I didn't care for school either. This is why the following is about to occur. Prepare yourself. I'll be gentle this time, but only because you're warming up to reading this novel. **If you don't like what's about to happen, please close this book and read elsewhere.** This book is loaded with this kind of activity and the tales concerning this activity only do what Cats do on a Tin Roof. These stories get a lot Hotter.

"We didn't do it last night."

"We did it the night before, didn't we?"

"No, we were at the Phillips until 10pm, then the babysitter wanted to stay and watch some movie."

"Oh ya. Well, in order to adhere to the standards and guidelines as suggested by Masters and Johnson, we should go at it at least every other day, which means we should do it right here, right now, on the cold tiles of the bathroom floor. You lie down first. Standard style is the preferred method as suggested by Masters."

"No, I want to be on top this time. You were on top last time. You should put your hairy buttocks on the cold tiles of the bathroom floor. Mine aren't nearly as insulated as yours."

"OK. Won't take long anyway. I'll count this time, too. But next time you're counting."

"I am aroused sufficiently. I am lubricated."

"I am elongated. I am inserting."

"Insertion is complete. Begin plucking."

"Counting. One. Two. Did you remember to take care of my shirts? Three."

Which is exactly the number of strokes it takes to get my 4 year old little girl to pound on the locked bathroom door of her parent's master bedroom. Don't be confused, while similar to the scenario involving an owl licking to the center of a tootsie roll pop, Murphy's Law Pertaining to Sex for Parents is more applicable. If you desire to get your child out of bed in the morning, do it in the bathroom. Your child will come knocking on the door when you get done with the third stroke like clockwork. Don't forget to bolt the door closed, otherwise, you might have some explaining to do.

CHAPTER 2

It's easier to get the dog to take a bath.

"Daddy and Mommy what are you guys doing in there?" Pound. Thump. Test the strength of the lock on the bathroom door.

"Mommy was pulling some hairs off daddy's backside, Kathy. We're just about done. Give us a minute."

"What da ya know, my Katherine O'Reilly turned into a Princess this morning. You have the loveliest morning coiffure I have ever gazed upon, my petite mademoiselle."

"Mommy, Daddy likes my bed head."

"Can I leave it like this for school, Daddy?"

"Kathy, bed heads are out of style. You're gonna have to take a bath so don't try to sneak a fast one by your Daddy."

"Mommy, can I leave my hair this way?"

My daughter always gets a second opinion when the first parent's response fails to yield a verdict she finds agreeable. In this case, it's appeal denied.

"Sure you can, Kat. Right after I help you take a bath Mom will help you put some Aqua Net glue, I mean hair spray, in your hair so you'll have a permanent bed head. Might take more than one bath to wash out, though."

"Daddy, will you help me take a bath?"

"Sure, precious. Daddy needs to finish shaving. Could you get the water started?"

I enjoy taking baths, or more precisely, showers. Kathy doesn't. Our dog, Pluto, enjoys taking a bath about as much as Kathy does. Let me give you an idea of what I have to go through to give the dog a bath. Food is out. The dog is too smart for the "give 'em some bait, so the dog will jump in a bucket of water" trick. At least when the weather is warm, giving Pluto a bath outside isn't so bad. The dog always wants outside, except when it's time for a bath. Don't ask me how, but the dog knows when bath time is near. I surmise my voice must inflect differently the words, "Come on boy, let's go outside." Well, I'm one up on the dog. I stand outside the doorway with one hand on the hose and the other on the doorbell. The dog comes running on the third ring every single time.

In order to get Kathy to take a bath, we have to pick the water toys, choose the correct color for today's bathroom towel, open up the shampoo bottle to see if there's enough to get the job done (She prefers to jump out of the tub only once during her bathing experience.), and, most importantly, get the bathing water temp just right. Lukewarm to my hands, as I kneel on the hard ceramic tiles of the bathroom floor, does not always correspond to the "correct to the tenth of a degree" temperature dictated by my girl's feet as she stands in the bathroom tub. Therein, lies the problem. Kathy dislikes, hates intensely is more like it, the sensation of going from warm air to cold water.

I bought thermometer thinking if I showed Kathy how to determine temperature, she could test the water herself. But my little Princess has told Daddy his hands do a better job. This makes sense since Daddy has also been told to hold the thermometer steadily underneath the faucet for no less than thirty seconds in order to obtain the most accurate reading possible.

My wife helps my daughter get dressed in the morning. By pure luck, I was fired from that job. A few months ago, I was given the duty of dressing the daughter as assigned by my beloved. I didn't think too much of dressing my little girl in white shoes, lime green pants, a pink polka dot shirt and accessorizing her outfit with an orange striped belt. Don't blame me, most of Pumpkin's clothes were dirty. I thought she looked darling. A few hours after I dropped Kathy off at the Montessori school, I got a call from the teacher. Some of the kids had teased my little one about her clothing attire. Now Princess doesn't want Daddy to help her pick her clothes, which is fine by me. I even need help getting dressed in the morning. That's one of the reasons I got married. Don't tell my wife I said that.

My little darling still prefers Daddy do the morning cooking. According to Kathy, no one in the world makes better cereal or toast or pancakes as good as Daddy does. I get a little help from General Mills, Pepperidge Farms and Nabisco. She still says I am the best pourer, jelly spreader, and cake flipper of all the Daddy's in the world which explains why Daddy makes breakfast and Kathy gets to sit at the kitchen table and watch.

Daddy is a pushover when Princess pulls one of her "Your'e the bestest" Daddy lines. Her favorite right now is "Daddy, you're the bestest Daddy in the whole world at tying shoelaces." Daddy can't dress, but he can still tie shoes. In general, the line goes as follows. Princess looks at Daddy with those darling little eyes and says, "Daddy, you're the bestest Daddy in the whole world, (that part is the line and now the punch) at doing something I don't want to do."

Daddy gets a great deal of joy from making the twinkle in my eyes something to eat in the morning, which happens to be toast today, because of what Kathy does at the table. Our dog Pluto fetches the newspaper from the driveway every morning. The dog doesn't run off when I let him out because Pluto knows Pluto's breakfast won't be poured from the can by me, something Pluto can't do, unless Pluto drops the paper next to the Master's feet in the kitchen every morning. Smart dog. He reminds me to make him something to eat. I used to take the paper from the floor, sit at the table with Kathy, and have some breakfast while I read the paper. I like my news the old fashioned way. (My wife won't let me put a computer on the dining room table.) Six months ago, I won't forget the day, the light of my life made me the proudest Daddy in the whole world. She picked up the paper, and gave it a shot on her own. She tried to read the paper to me just like her Daddy read aloud to her. She didn't get one word right. According to her, the headline of the St. Louis Post Dispatch dated June 1, 2016, read "Mommy deals a decisive blow to Kathy's hiccup dilemma." One of the headlines from the sports section read, "Me and Katy played

Barbie yesterday at Ken's house. Tomorrow play is at John's place."

I figured what she needed to get a word right was a picture with the words attached. So I started her off with Family Circus in the funnies section. Now she can read all the funnies except Dilbert. She says Dilbert isn't very funny. I think she's trying to tease her Daddy. My Princess got that character attribute from her mother. Daddy thinks Dilbert is hilarious because Dilbert is just like Daddy's life. I forget to tell you what I do for a living. In brief, for now, I'm a computer nerd, and the Dilbert cartoon is a nerd's idea of humor.

There is a drawback to a four-year old child reading the morning paper Daddy didn't think about. She can read the words on the front page, but she doesn't understand concepts like war in the Middle East or drug lords in South America or starvation in Africa or murder in America. The questions she asks. Daddy has to think too much in the morning, or any time of the day, to give an answer to such questions, as if, there is an answer to such questions. I try to make an effort to grab the front page first, and hope she is content to read the funnies. For now, it's working. When she starts asking for the front page I'm going to assign my wife the morning breakfast duties.

Ya right. Who am I kidding? My wife takes ten times longer in the morning to get ready for work, and that's generous. Maybe I'll get her one of those "Morning Makeovers" that Boncoeur just put out on the market. When I tell her, "I'm gonna get you one of those Morning Makeover kits," she answers, "I don't want a computer putting on my makeup." I might get her one for Christmas, but I'm sure she'll exchange the device for more clothes. Maybe Mother's Day. That will give me plenty of time to warm her up to the new high tech idea.

"Kathy, what are you doing!"

"I'm pouring milk on the floor just like in the cartoon, Daddy. See, look at the funny."

"Katherine O'Reilly. If someone jumped off a bridge would you jump off of it too! Now I've got to clean up the mess you made."

"Daddy in the cartoon cleans it up to, Daddy."

My Princess can do no wrong. Just because my four-year old can read the paper doesn't make her anything less than a four-year old who learns by imitating.

"Kathy, why don't you get some paper towels and help your Father wipe up the milk you spilt."

"Honey, I'm done. It's 7:30. You're going to miss your flight, if you don't hurry."

"Daddy, I'm sorry. I didn't mean to make you late for your plane ride."

"Don't worry Pumpkin. Daddy won't miss his flight. Can you help me by cleaning up the floor by yourself?"

"OK."

Kids. You got a love them. I'm not awfully late. All I need to do is hop on my business suit, and check the computer before I put it in my briefcase.

We've got a huge master bedroom closet. Not that I need the space for my stuff. The closet is mainly for my better half, as fitting, her garments occupy most of the closet. When we purchased the house two years ago, we had an oral agreement. I would get the left half of the closet and she would get the right half. 50-50 done the middle. But my clothes barely occupied a quarter of my half of the closet when we moved in. I told her I needed the room for the golf clubs I always wanted to get. She told me I told her I didn't like golf. My better half has steadily consumed all of the closet space and I still don't have any clubs. I dare not say a word. I don't want to move into a bigger house, which, incidentally, has a larger master bedroom closet, and, consequently, a greater mortgage payment.

My closet space is limited to the lower left back corner. I have six white business shirts, six pair of slacks, and three business suits, one black, one dark blue, and one brown. I've got a couple of shirts I hardly ever wear like the Hawaiian shirt my wife bought me when we went to Hawaii. She made me wear one for the resort luau.

I've also have a small personal refrigerator, hidden behind my clothes in the corner, for one of my "closet habits." Behind the fridge, is a shoebox containing paraphernalia for my other habit. I keep both in the closet for a reason. My two kids don't know about my two habits.

Excuse me. I need to get dressed. I've got a plane to catch.

CHAPTER 3
John's past is locked in the closet.

John O'Reilly looked for his white shirts. He had six white shirts. One was hanging in the closet. He sniffed under the armpit of the shirt. No way. He looked in the closet. No white shirts in the closet were his.

"Wife, where are my clean white shirts!" No reply.

He breathed deeply. He looked again. The blue shirt was clean. His blue suit was clean. He was going to be late. He reached for the shirt. He took another breath to inhale a greater quantity of air.

He was three months out, or one quarter away from being out of business. If he didn't get new business, and he couldn't milk his one existing contract anymore, he could make payroll for the dozen employees of O'Reilly & Associates three more times. This wasn't the first time he'd been in such a predicament. He'd been "three months out, and a quarter short" a few times before, but this time was different except for one other time. He had only one potential business client lined up this time, which was ninety nine less than he would have liked to have knocking on his door. He had to get this business from the client he was going to meet today, or start doing some serious marketing. Only the idea of spending the next three months on the phone and trying to get his employees to do something else besides program a computer, namely become marketeers, made this solitary prospect appear more hopeful.

The conversation with the IBM representative, not even a programmer, had been brief, just ten minutes. The rep had simply asked him Friday if he was available for contract work. What contract work? The rep wouldn't say. O'Reilly assumed the rep didn't even know what the job entailed; however, IBM wanted him to go to Boca Raton, Florida that day. The job must be urgent, and urgent jobs, he knew, pay well.

He reached for the blue shirt, and another breath, a breath he had no control over, resulted in no intake of air. He had seen this blue shirt before. He remembered. John O'Reilly would never forget, no matter how hard he tried.

John looked at the appointment card. Tuesday, August 18, 1998. The appointment time, 5:30pm, was barely legible. He stepped into his apartment at 5:00pm. He had left work fifteen minutes early. He hadn't asked to take off early but the store was empty and the manager on duty was in the break room having a smoke. John didn't like going into the break room. The smoke concentrated easily in the small room, not much larger than a closet in size. He would come in a few minutes early tomorrow to make up for the time. He needed to leave his apartment by 5:05pm or else.

Two months ago he had showed up at the doctor's office at a quarter till six. There was no one there. The office was locked. The therapist mentioned he had waited almost an hour for John to make the appointment. As John was his last of the day, Bill Mueller had decided to leave.

The time was a 5:09pm as he locked the door to his apartment. He got in his truck. He checked for money in his wallet. Empty. He hurried back to his apartment. He was in luck. He had two fives in his money jar. The office manager frowned on showing up with no money.

He checked his watch as he stepped into the waiting room of Dr. Syed, Psychotherapy Provided by a Physician, as the sign read on the door. The time was 5:41pm.

The office manager greeted him. "John. Sign in."

John filled in the last line on the sign-in sheet.

"It's ten dollars." John handed over the two fives. He read the sign on the opaque window as it quickly closed and blurred the image of the manager sitting at the sign-in desk. FULL PAYMENT IS EXPECTED UPON SERVICES BEING RENDERED.

John suspected full payment was more than ten dollars, but he was never asked to pay more. The fear of having to pay more, if he were to ask how much a session cost, kept him from raising the question. Ten dollars twice a month was twenty dollars. He did the math. 35 hours times 7 bucks an hour plus 30 hours times 6 bucks an hour was 1700 dollars a month minus taxes took him down to 1400 dollars. Rent was 500. Down to 900. Food was 200. Down to 700. Paying for gas, insurance, and balance on the car loan was another 200. With five hundred bucks a months, or 125 per week, he could buy whatever he wanted, minus another twenty bucks.

The door to the hallway leading to the therapist's office buzzed. As it unlocked, Bill Mueller and Bill Mueller's 4:30 stepped out. A young lady, about John's age, said goodbye to Bill. John did not look at her nor did she at John.

"I'll be with you in just a minute, John."

The door buzzed again at a few minutes past six.

"Sorry, John. I was writing some notes on the previous case history and got carried away in the details."

John took a seat in the chair closest to the door.

The therapist took a seat behind his glass desk. He unloosened his tie.

"These twelve hour days are hard. Don't mind my shirt John, I split coffee on it today. This is my favorite blue shirt, too."

John looked at the stain adjacent to the therapist's pants. The pants weren't stained.

"Tough working at the prison today. They had to drug up one of my manic depressives. I was stuck in the same cell with him for ten minutes before the nurses could get him sedated. Then I had to spend a whole hour at the ward trying to talk to a Schizophrenic staring at a wall. Completely catatonic. Boring! What a day. How about you?"

"I had a tough time getting here."

"How's work going?"

"Which job?"

Mueller looked at the paperwork on his desk. "Best Buy. You're a computer technician. How's the computer world nowadays?"

"It was slow today. I had a few calls in the morning. Nothing special."

"You know, I got a problem with my Pentitulum laptop."

"Ya."

"It says something on the screen about a fatal expecting error then I can't save my word document."

"I'm not a programmer. I don't know the answer."

"Thought I'd ask. You mind if I smoke."

"No. I guess not."

Mueller glanced at the papers on his desk. "How's Schnucks?"

"I'll have two years in next week. I'm up for a raise." Pause. "I think it's a quarter an hour." Pause. "I think that's standard for the union, but I'm not sure." Pause. "That's what one of the other stockers, my friend Mike, said he got."

"Have you made any new friends since we talked?"

John spoke quietly to the ground, "No."

"Have you tried?"

John didn't reply.

"John, you need to make some more friends. Just go into a bar and start talking to people. It's easy."

"Ya." Pause. John looked as if he was about to speak, but he didn't. He looked at his watch.

"Are you still continuing you're Prozac therapy?"

He nodded his head. "I take one in the morning." He began to talk again but stuttered slightly. He tried again. "I have to go. My shift starts at seven. I was. I can't be late for work this time."

"Ok, John. Let's make your appointment at the same time two weeks from now. Is that good for you?"

"Ya."

"Here, let me write the appointment time down on a card for you."

"That's ok. I'll change the date on the one I have."

"I'll see you in two weeks, John."

"I see you." John searched for a word. "when?"

"In two weeks."

16

The lock on the door buzzed. John was free to go. He hurried to his truck. He opened the door to his truck. He would change shirts here. He reached for the white shirt. Schnucks stockers wore a white shirt.

John O'Reilly reached. He tried to reach again. His hands couldn't grasp the shirt.

"Here honey."

He felt a reassuring grip on his shoulder. The hand slowly moved to the back of his neck and gently massaged the tension from his muscles. He relaxed.

"I just finished pressing one of you're white shirts. It's clean."

CHAPTER 4

Don't cry over spilled milk.

To catch a plane or not to catch a plane and help his little darling. Kathy had tried the best she could but had made more of a mess than less of a mess. Where there was once spilt milk, now a monument of paper towels stood. An assortment of cleaners was strewn across the kitchen counter. Two bottles were empty. One bottle showed a strange concoction of three blended colors. In the corner of the kitchen sat John O'Reilly's little four-year old girl. In her left hand was cleaner A and in her right hand was cleaner B. Straddled between the child's legs were half a roll of paper towels. Held by her feet was a single paper towel. With scientific precision she was spraying the paper towel with an equal amount from each of the two bottles. After momentary examination she tossed the paper towel toward the monument.

Kathy looked up to her father and smiled. "Look Daddy, I'm seeing which stuff from the bottle is better absorbed by Bounty, the picker upper."

John did not smile back, nor did he give an indication of displeasure on his face. He stared at the bottles on the kitchen counter and picked up the two empty ones, one in each hand, on the counter. With one foot he stepped on the lever to lift the lid to the trashcan. Why, of all days, did his innocent little Bo Peep have to turn into Dr. Strangelove, the mad scientist? The lid flipped open. He peered at the items in the trashcan. Why did he have to hold two empty bottles in his hands and dig through the trash today, of all days?

CHAPTER 5

He needed what he did not have.

John didn't expect to be digging in a dumpster at 6am on a Saturday morning. Someone on the Friday shift had not done his job. Friday's boxes, the byproduct of last night's stocking of new inventory, had been pitched in the trash without breaking them down first. The dumpster was full, but mostly with dead air space. A fresh truckload of produce had arrived this morning, a day late. John was given the task of making room in the dumpster for the produce boxes. His former boss would have told the evening crew to get all of the boxes out of the trash, break down the boxes, and fill the dumpster properly. The new assistant manager, Chuck, a chubby guy in his late twenties, had not done as such. John had stocked the shelves last night as he watched Chuck spend all evening chatting with the check out girls. John didn't work the Saturday morning shift at the Schnucks supermarket on a regular basis. He preferred to work the afternoon shift, spending the morning doing whatever errands he needed to get done, get a haircut, do the laundry, read a book at the library, etc. His old boss knew this. John did not need to make a request. But this new assistant manager had made this week's schedule, and John had failed to fill out a schedule request form. Rather than ask for a shift change earlier in the week, John just accepted it. With each reach into the dumpster, he wished he had asked for a schedule change.

At one o'clock, John felt tired. One more hour to go he told himself. He had gotten off work at 10pm last night, went to bed at 11pm, but had not fallen asleep till 3am. He stared at his alarm clock, watching the numbers cycle from 0 to 59 over and over again. As he stood on a catwalk thirty feet above the backroom floor, he strained to count the number of cartons he had stacked to help out the other stocker doing inventory.

The "holding area," referred to by management what stockers called the "backroom", was cramped. Two truckloads of boxed produce occupied nearly the entire floor space. The entire back wall of tiered industrial shelving was full of boxes containing everything from canned asparagus to cases of motor oil. John stood precariously on the "third floor" walkway adjacent to the topmost shelf struggling to cram more cartoons of cigarettes onto the shelf.

"Yo! John boy!"

John quickly turned around. His head spun. The new assistant manager and two new manager look a likes, stood on the floor directly underneath him.

"Hey be careful up there! What da ya want me to have to do? Call 911?"

John put his hand on the railing.

"Ya."

The manager clasped his hands around his mouth to extend his voice. "You want to make some extra money today? Fill the afternoon shift?"

"No. I'm not interested."

"Hey, listen. We're short in produce today. We've got to get these crates of produce out on the floor. So how about it?"

"I can't." John strained to recall the assistant manager's name. "I'm tired. Sorry, Charlie."

"Hey John! I'm the one doing performance appraisals for stockers this month. You're not showing a team attitude. Understood!"

John didn't know why he took the indignation he took that day. He didn't reply. He didn't care anymore. Caring would require feeling, and the only sensation his body could produce at the moment was the state of exhaustion. Nothing could be said to him that could do him any harm. This state of mind, totally impervious to the sensation of pain, brought upon by an uncaring overweight boss would change his life. For in life, sometimes an injustice can produce justice. One wrong can make one right. For John O'Reilly, today would be the beginning of a new life.

He first saw the man crouched over the bookrack in aisle thirteen. John had an hour break, the next shift started at 2pm, ending at 10pm. He could have walked to his apartment and napped. If he did, he would have walked back only in his sleep. He tried to find a comfortable crate to nap upon. He had done so in the past, but the hustle in the backroom inhibited him from slumbering soundly. The sweltering afternoon summer heat and humidity kept the thought of snoozing outside out of his mind. He decided to go to the magazine rack and read lightly if he could, or at the least stare at a few pictures to keep awake. John opened a Computer Shopper as the man grabbed a romance novel from the bookrack. Odd, John thought, that a man, an old man, would want to read a book intended for women.

They were only five feet apart but the man gave no notice to John being in his presence. The old man, maybe in his seventies John surmised after taking a second glance, was intensely focused on the storyline on the back cover of the novel he held. He flipped through the pages, putting a finger on one page, then a finger on another, so as to make a place marker. His crooked fingers matched his age. The skin was wrinkled and sagged greatly to make a crevice, one at each joint. Wherever his fingers had been, he had put them there often. More peculiar was the shape of the man's balding head, with thin wisps of hair on the top of his dome. Apparently the man had not received a haircut in sometime. The old man appeared from John's vantage point to have two protrusions jutting from his scalp, horns much the same as a billy goat. The man chewed as he turned to the last page. He reread the pages his fingers had bookmarked.

"This old maid doesn't know how to write a love story. Crap. Complete dog doo-doo. I can write better than this standing on my hands."

The old man didn't look up. He put the book down to pick up another book that contained a partially eaten donut serving as a place marker.

"This donut taste like shit. Hey kid. Ya you. Are you a baker boy?"

21

John tried to act as if he was looking further down the book aisle. He had been caught looking directly at the man. A look of bewilderment took upon his face. His body got a shot of adrenaline. He was awake.

"No, I'm a stocker," as he shook his head fervently.

"If you tell your manager I'm eatin' donuts, I'm gonna tell him all twelve of these donuts taste like cow crap. That's why I haven't eatin' all of one yet. Got it. And since I haven't eatin' a donut from this dozen, I'm not paying for none of 'em. Got it!"

John looked at the donuts, each partially eaten, and each wrapped in a romance novel. He could tell they were romance novels from the pictures on the cover. Each book cover was different but all had a common attribute. Each had the picture of a shirtless man with a voluptuous woman clutched in his arms.

"I don't work in the bakery department. I don't even know who the bakery manager is."

"Then what the hell are you lookin' at? It's a free country. I can read anything I want to if I want to. Skedaddle!"

John scurried back to the employees lounge. The time was 1:48pm. He could clock back in four minutes. As he stocked produce the rest of the afternoon only one thought kept him awake. Why was an old man eating donuts in the store? And the same thought helped him dream through the day. Why would this man say he could write better romance novels standing on his hands?

He couldn't keep his eyes open at nine o'clock, but he made it to nine thirty. At nine forty five he sat down in the backroom. He told himself he would close his eyes for just a second. When he opened his eyes to look at his watch the time was ten thirty. He jumped up. He could clock out at no later than ten past ten or management would ask why he left so late, especially on a Saturday night. John walked past the break room table to the clock machine and ran his finger over the list of timecards looking for his name. He inserted his card. The machine did not make the stamping noise he normally heard. He checked the card. The timestamp read 10:09 PM. He didn't remember clocking out. How did he do this in his sleep? He didn't give this much thought. He was free to go home and for once he wasn't tired.

What would he do with his free time? He walked to the aisle with the computer magazines. Which one? PC Magazine or Computer Shopper. He couldn't buy both. PC Magazine had an article on computer networking he was interested in. It wouldn't take him long to read the article. He could save some money by reading the article in the store. He got in line, the only check out counter open on a Saturday night at Schnucks, with a Computer Shopper, containing over four hundred pages of computer parts for sale, under one arm and a loaf of bread under the other.

"Hi John!"

"Hi Jovita."

"I caught you!"

"Huh?"

"In the backroom sleeping. Don't worry. I didn't tell Chuck."

"Thanks."

"So what ya doing tonight?"

"I'm going to go through this magazine looking for the cheapest computer parts I can find, eat a couple of peanut butter and jelly sandwiches, and get some sleep. I didn't sleep well last night."

"I've got some nighttime cough syrup if you want some."

"Thanks Jovita, I've got something from a." Pause. "to help me sleep."

"You don't have to pay me if you don't want to." Jovita smiled. "I won't tell. Chuck is outside taking a smoke break. Besides, everyone else does."

John looked at the ten he held in his hand. He hesitated. "I couldn't." He paused. He looked at Jovita. "I wouldn't sleep well tonight."

"I was just trying to help out. Your total is six dollars and a penny."

"I don't have a penny."

"That's OK. I've got one."

"I'll see you later, Jovita."

"See ya. Bye-bye John. Talk to you later!"

He wasn't tired as he approached the intersection of Clayton Road and Woods Mill. After crossing on foot tiredness overtook his body again. This was the only busy intersection he had to transverse. The rest of the walk home would be leisurely.

He passed an Amoco gas station and walked up the stairs to the back half of the shopping center across the street from Schnucks. The front half facing Woods Mill Road had a Great Clips where he usually got his haircuts, and a few restaurants. John had been inside each establishment one time apiece to apply for a job. In the back half of the strip mall facing Clayton Road was a dry cleaners. John had been there once. The back half parking lot was full. A bar and grill, the Country Club, was in full swing.

He could hear the band playing inside. As he walked by, he glanced at the neon sign, Budweiser, centered in the window. He stopped to watch a couple enter the establishment. He continued his walk home alone when he heard the music intensify. At the end of the parking lot, next to a vacated store that was once a flooring business, was a fence. The fence was not continuous. A few of the planks were conveniently missing. This opening allowed John to gain entrance to the adjacent apartment complex, Village Green Apartments.

He had walked by the dumpster next to his apartment building labeled 14452 a thousand times. He had lifted the lid to that dumpster a hundred times. Something so commonplace in his environment would warrant no more attention than an instantaneous glance, but this brief glance gave reason to look at the dumpster indefinitely. Two feet dangled in the air. Attached to these feet were two limbs protruding from underneath the lid of the dumpster. He could see the belly, rather round, which supported the individual who may, or may not, have been headless. A voice echoed from the container.

"This stinks. Dammit Mary and her bastard son!"

Whoever this person was, he was not jolly, even though he, the voice was definitely of a man, gave every semblance to being stuck atop a chimney in the latter part of December. John grabbed the man's feet. With this brace the man was able to pull his upper torso upright.

The man turned to look at his helper. "What the hell you looking at?"

John was holding the feet of the same man he had seen this afternoon at the supermarket. "I was just trying to help."

"Well, I don't need your help. Haven't you ever seen some one diggin' in the trash before, baker boy!"

The man recognized him. John returned a cowardly gesture, "I thought you were stuck so."

"I wasn't stuck kid. I was trying to get my bottles."

John nodded his head but said nothing. His back slouched and his shoulders shrunk.

"Say kid, you're taller than me. You're about six one, aren't ya?"

John nodded.

"I'm five foot six when I got on sneakers. You wanna help? See those bottles at the bottom stuck underneath that box?" The man pointed into the dumpster.

"Ya."

"Get those bottles for me all right guy."

John reached into the trash. The bottles were just out of arms reach. He had already stepped into trash once today. No activity would he partake in today that would lesson the value of his self. He looked down at the old man standing next to him.

"Give me just a second to get your bottles."

"Okay kid. Be careful, all right," the old man appeared to take an interest in John's well being.

John got in the trash and grabbed the two bottles. The bottles were each about half full, give or take a drink or two. He read the label on one of the bottles to himself, "GlenLivet. Aged 12 years. Pure malt scotch whiskey distilled since 1824."

"Thanks kid. You're the greatest." The old man anxiously grabbed the two jars away from John. He gazed contently at the bottles he held.

"My precious, my sweet precious." He cradled the bottles in his arms. "I promise I'll never ever leave you anywhere close to the trashcan where that wicked, two-timin', no good, filthy, more rotton than the eggs I ate this mornin', more yello' than the eggs I just got done barfin' up maid of mine. That bitch. I'll never let her throw out my garbage again, I promise, forever and ever, I do promise. I swear on my fourth ex-wife soon to be grave, too, my dear precious I'll never release you from my tender embrace again."

The old man looked up at John as he lowered himself out of the dumpster.

"Kid. Got a thought for ya. Take a look at this here bottle. Is it half full or half empty? That is the question. What's the answer kid?"

"I don't know."

"Okay. Okay. Okay." The man said hurriedly. "They half full now, but they be all empty an hour from now 'cause it's Saturday night meanin' itsa wholelotta drinkin' time, 'cause gotta do 'tll Monday. Gotta go. See ya later."

John didn't get much sleep that night. He flipped through the pages of his Computer Shopper till the early morning light. As he looked at the prices on various computer parts he wondered who was the man he had met today.

CHAPTER 6

He didn't have a pack on the packed plane.

"Daddy, what are you doing Daddy!" Kathy spread her words with a spray of anxiety.

"What Pumpkin?"

"Daddy, you shouldn't put those bottles in that trashcan. They belong in the recycling bin." Kathy's concern gave her face sternness. "You're polluting the environment, Daddy. Do not put the bottles in the trash."

"Sorry, Kathy. I don't know what I was thinking. I didn't mean to do it on purpose." John walked over to the recycling bin and tossed the two containers. He thought he heard heels on the kitchen linoleum.

"John! You're gonna miss your plane if we don't hurry."

He spun around to see his wife standing near the garage door. "Okay. Okay. Okay. You don't have to yell."

His wife was twenty feet away from him. In her heels she looked in her twenties to him. She was a blonde, with hair slightly longer than shoulder length. Her hairstyle was simple as her locks were straight, but a red clip holding her hair back gave her hairstyle a look of elegance. Which did he enjoy more? Watching her remove the clip from her hair as she tossed her head slightly to let her blonde threads rest on her shoulders or to see her tresses within a hair's width of her business attire? She had on a red skirt and matching blazer, but the thought of her not wearing anything gave fire to his heart. She was shorter than him by half a foot. The heels gave her the extra inch needed for her eyes to meet his. She was not petite. Her bosom was full, but not overly so. Her body was trim. The calves gave full sight to her fitness as she wore no hose, and the skirt hid any indication her legs were of a 43-year old woman sagging slightly above the knees.

"Honey, I've still got a couple of hairs I need to get plucked off my back." John pointed towards his shoulder as Kathy watched.

"Knock it off. You had your chance this morning."

"Daddy, I'll chop the hairs off your back."

"See honey. My daughter will take the time to help me out."

"Ya. Whatever. Let's go."

"Can we take the fast car, Daddy?"

"Nope. We're taking my car," Mrs. O'Reilly interjected.

"But I don't wanna go in the slow car."

"Tough luck. Get in Mommy's car now or I'm gonna strap you in the child seat myself. Better yet. I'll tie you on the hood like a dear."

"Daddy, do I have to?"

"Yes dear, mind your Mom. Playtime's over."

The three O'Reilly's got into their 2014 four door Chevrolet Cavalier. The time on the dashboard clock read 7:45. If traffic was good, John would just make his 9am flight to Boca Raton, Florida. He turned around in the front passenger seat to make sure his daughter had buckled herself in. A calculator stuck out from his four-year old's backpack.

"Stop the car. I forgot my laptop."

He hurried inside to the den adjacent to the front door of the O'Reilly residence. His laptop was already packed, including his infrared linked CDR-ROM2 drive he would need for his business meeting this afternoon in Boca. O'Reilly was nervous. He had made such presentations, selling the services and abilities of his company, to prospective clients before but this one was important. His desire to satisfy his craving for one was even more important. He hurried into the master bedroom, dropping the laptop at the entrance to the adjoining walk-in closet. He opened up the shoebox hidden behind the refrigerator.

"I know I had a few smokes left just yesterday."

The box he held in his hand was empty. He was out of cigarettes. He would get some at the airport if he had time.

"Got everything?"

"Yup."

"Are you sure? I try to keep my u-turns with a child in the backseat down to one a day."

John smiled. "Yes. I'm sure."

He needed only one thing more than a smoke. O'Reilly needed to sleep, and the constant stop and go rush to work morning traffic produced the necessary rhythm to induce his body to sleep. He was free to relax. His wife was doing the driving.

"Kathy don't pull on the hairs on Daddy's neck. Daddy needs to sleep. OK?"

"But Mommy we're almost at school and I want Daddy to kiss me good-bye."

"You can kiss your Daddy good-bye while he's sleeping."

Mrs. O'Reilly pulled up to the student drop off zone of the Hope Montessori School. Cathy reached over the front seat and kissed her dad on the cheek.

"Bye honey. Drive safe to work. I'll call you on the flight home to let you know how the presentation went."

"Bye Daddy."

John O'Reilly raised his hand in a motion like a child waving bye-bye. His eyes visibly turned underneath his eyelids. He was sound asleep.

"John. Honey. We're here. We're at the airport." Mrs. O'Reilly spoke in a soothing voice.

"Thanks for dropping me off. I'll let you know how the presentation went."

"Honey, we're at Lambert Field. You need to wake up."

John opened one eye. The other eye remained shut. "You already dropped me off."

"John O'Reilly you'll miss your flight."

"I'm awake. Thanks for the ride, gorgeous."

O'Reilly shut the door to the Cavalier. His nap renewed his vigor. Mr. O'Reilly was the CEO of a Fortune 500 company taking his first step from a limousine to shake hands with a potential client whose business could reap profits in the billions. He opened both eyes.

"John, call me on your way back to St. Louis so I'll know when to pick you up. Good luck, honey. I love you." She leaned out the window to give him a peck on the cheek.

John waved good-bye to his wife as she drove away. He felt like he was worth a billion smackeroos until he stepped into the airport. At the beginning of the line of the ticket counter he checked the time. Fifteen minutes to spare. At the end of the line, he was five minutes late. Someone at the counter had done a bit of theatrics. He didn't hear the dialogue, but the hand waving the United Airlines employee was doing behind the counter had been comical. O'Reilly wasn't concerned about being late. The ticket had already been purchased over the Internet. He needed only pick it up at the counter.

"That flight has already been boarded, sir, and the gate closed."

"But I've been standing in your line, United 'we all stand together in line forever' Airlines, for the past twenty minutes!"

"I'm sorry, sir. Someone flunked the Terrorist Test."

"What?"

"When I asked him if he had associated with or had any association with any terrorist or terrorist organization he said 'Less than a hundred today.' Well, I got him. He should have said 'no' just like everyone else. See the guy over there talking with the police?"

"Well, I need to get to Boca Raton, Florida by noon." O'Reilly stared. "By noon today, sir." He added the 'sir' to cover for the belittlement, not so gently, he had given to the man.

"Let's see. I do have a 9:30 flight to Miami. Let's see. I do have an aisle seat in coach. Will this be adequate, sir?"

"Coach is what I was on before I got on your stage."

"Round trip will be $958."

"What! I paid $318 for the 9am flight." O'Reilly recalled why he had chosen the 9am flight over the 9:30. Someone had bit the seat of his pants and chewed it into a billion nibbles. O'Reilly acted like he was looking for some change in his wallet.

"I'll take it. Get me a rental car for today, too. Only today, ticket master."

"Yes, sir."

John took the ticket from the guy behind the counter. "Entertainment is expensive, nowadays, isn't it?" he said with no attempt to cover a hale of sarcasm.

He didn't have time to buy a pack of cigarettes at the terminal. He couldn't afford to miss his flight, for the second time.

His aisle seat provided much needed additional area. Since the man to his side was very obtuse O'Reilly leaned toward the aisle at a pronounced angle. He kicked three times to charm his briefcase into hiding in the storage basin underneath his seat. He had given up on trying the overhead storage. Everyone on the plane had taken their share of overhead storage. He looked at the line for the restroom at the rear of the plane. One more kick convinced the laptop to stay put down below, enough so he could remove his legs from the walkway. Five people were standing in line at the restroom, four of which just walked past him. He counted the empty seats. There were five. This plane was packed with the fat man beside him counting as two sardines.

"Sir, your briefcase isn't stored properly for takeoff."

O'Reilly winged his best angelic smile for the flight attendant. "I tried to store it up above, but I couldn't find any space." His face turned to one who was overcome with anxiety. "I tried to."

"Let me check for you."

The stewardess checked every overhead compartment thoroughly. She vanished behind a curtain concealing the fist class seating.

"We don't have any space. You can leave your briefcase beneath your seat," she said with a Florence Nightingale grin. "What's a businessman like you traveling second class for anyway?"

O'Reilly smiled, "I travel coach so I can inspire to be a first class businessman. If I sat up front, I would have nothing to achieve."

The stewardess smiled as she tried to conceal a giggle.

"And an aisle seat near the restroom is what my stomach demands even though the rest of me wants a double wide seat with a doggie bag."

She laughed. "I would let you in business seating but they're all full," she said with a look of attentiveness.

"Don't worry about the barf bag. I'm flying on an empty stomach. My wife didn't cook me breakfast this morning."

She smiled as she placed a pillow under his neck. O'Reilly hadn't asked for one. The stewardess also politely offered, while he was using his laptop computer, if he would like some coffee. She made the offer each time she carried the coffee pot to the first class business section. The businessman returned a smile each time. He was flying first class in a single wide seat.

CHAPTER 7

When you're staring at a plank of wood, look for a hole to put the key in.

John O'Reilly's meeting with International Business Machines was at 1pm. He didn't take offense to not being invited to a noon lunch. His stomach didn't tolerate meals very well after a flight. Being invited to lunch would have made his excursion from St. Louis to Miami all the more hurried. O'Reilly was able to relax on the flight and get some work done. A thirty-minute warm up allowed him to transform the art of pitching to a science of selling.

His business plan was simple. He always stated it in some form or fashion within the first minute of his presentation. "We fix what's broke," would do nicely for an after lunch show. He would tell a joke about what business people do when the coffee doesn't take effect after a lunch meal as an eye opener. He always went to great lengths to make sure he did not say or give any impression of saying, "We fix what you've broken." He'd learned the hard way in his first year of business when you start by pointing the finger you usually end up getting the finger pointed back at you with no paycheck in the other customer's hand. Never ever say the four letter word "your."

"When you tell the customer, 'it's your problem', our problem will be no problem to fix for the customer. And if it's no problem for us to fix we're not going to get paid much," he would say to his associates.

The goal of the introduction, as John O'Reilly stated to his associates, was to break the "closeness" barrier.

"If the customer doesn't see you as their friend within the first five minutes you might as well walk out the door because you're not going to get their business." He would reiterate the statement, " Only after making sure I'm sitting on the same side of the table as the customer, not on the far end of a three foot wide plank of oak veneer, do I tell the customer my credentials and how I can use my skills to solve OUR problem."

Now came the sell. In his fifth year of business, he had plenty of pitches to choose from. O'Reilly & Associates had solved a General Motors parts distribution software glitch that made fourteen manufacturing plants non-operational for ten days. All plants were back online in 48 hours. O'Reilly & Associates was able to patch an antiquated database program used by ToysRUs to maintain inventory, overhaul it, and integrate it into an existing sales ordering system. As a result, ToysRUs went "pure virtual" over the Internet, converting all retail space to warehouse space, only four months after the contract start date. ToysRUs was so pleased with the work he got a $5000 Gift Certificate as a bonus.

His potential clients got a chuckle out of, "All I can see from wall to wall in my daughter's room are Barbies. If I'm lucky I only trip on one or two Kens in the doorway."

Sometimes the snooty anti-family business types would put a frown, not a smile, upon their face on bringing up family matters at a business meeting. He would mention the work O'Reilly & Associates did for the Missouri Department of Motor Vehicles. No one with a personal computer and a phone line had to step into a DMV branch office to renew their license plates. O'Reilly & Associates had written the Internet software. That statement usually got the snooty types nodding in affirmation. He would continue with the subsequent work the Missouri IRS had asked O'Reilly to do. All Missouri taxpayers, including O'Reilly, could handle every concern pertaining to property and personal income tax issues over the Internet.

"I haven't been to an IRS office, filled out a paper return, or talked with an IRS agent in three years, and I've haven't been arrested yet." The snooty types opened their mouths wide to sink their teeth into this line.

Once the potential client was at the table, doing a deal was all too easy. O'Reilly & Associates was comprised of himself and twelve other crackerjack coders to redo, fix, solve, or invent what some crackpot programmer at the company he was making the presentation had screwed up. O'Reilly's specialty was database optimization and web interfacing to backend data warehouses of stored information. Whether the ailing database was ancient dbase code, Oracle 13.5, or a proprietary in-house relational database he could make it better. He'd been doing this kind of work, a computer specialty akin to a doctor specializing in cardiovascular surgery, for fifteen years. He'd seen every type of malfunctioning computer program, and in turn, uncoded a great deal of botched computer code. His twelve associates rounded out the team to cover areas of the computer spectrum where his expertise was lacking, or better said, somewhat lacking. Combined all together, he and his associates had over two hundred years of computer know how. If he got this far in the presentation, a deal, with a jackpot forthcoming, was done.

Sometimes they would ask how a young man like him, they frequently told him he looked thirty five, managed to govern a team of old timer programmers. Only then would he tell them the average age of his staff was 28, and that was including him, an over the hill 40 year programmer.

Looking into eyes of disbelief he would say, "Most of my coders cut their teeth on a joystick, and could hold a keyboard before they could pick up a pencil." That one never failed to get them to sign on the dotted line.

When he first started his company in 2010 he did over one hundred sales presentations but made only ten deals. Of these, only three netted over ten thousands dollars in receipts.

In baseball terminology, which O'Reilly frequently employed when coaching his associates, " My rookie year, I had over a hundred at bats, got ten hits, and only three of those were for extra bases. Didn't hit a one out of the park. Believe me, when the Creve Couer, Missouri Chamber of Commerce was handing out Rookie Business of the Year Awards they didn't even bat an eye when they looked my way. But I stuck with it, and in my fourth season, just two years ago, I batted.400 with five at bats and the two I hit, I hit out of the park. That's where I got the money to get that Cray Super Computer sitting in the basement of my house. I made so much, in fact, after I paid FedEx same day delivery from Las Alamos, my wife made me buy a bigger house with a bigger basement. And that's when, during the move to my present hacienda, the Cray took a crap. I've been trying to get it to work ever since."

He liked to tell this story, which had some truth, of why he had a broken down Cray Super Computer in his house where there was once a cellar of wine casks. The true story, he had bought it from a computer junk dealer he had met at a convention in Los Angeles for $200, didn't sound nearly as good.

He had made seventeen presentations this year. Sixteen times he had made the big swing and struck out each time. Granted, trying to hit the long ball, going for the multi million dollar contract, would result in a lower on base percentage. The slump had changed his attitude. He needed to get on base, even a walk would do. His other associates hadn't faired any better. This was to be expected. They were green at doing presentations to potential customers like he was his rookie year. Only Mac, who had been with O'Reilly for three years, the longest of his associates, had been able to line up a good prospect. Unfortunately, business with this California startup wasn't going to materialize until the third quarter of next year, a quarter too late. He had to get some business to keep the company afloat through late spring. If Mac's prospect panned gold O'Reilly and a hundred Associates would have a research and development contract for a solid year. O'Reilly could see the Miami stadium, home of the pro baseball team, the Florida Marlins. The boss needed to show the boys of summer how to slug one out of the park.

This was his tenth time he had driven from Miami International to Boca Raton, Florida. He even knew of a convenience mart where grabbing a pack of cigarettes was off the beaten track by only a second. He didn't feel he had the time for such a pit stop, yet he wasn't so rushed he had to pretend I-95 was the extended version of Indianapolis International Speedway. He couldn't decide what lane to take. But O'Reilly had already put his Hertz rental car on auto pilot and, as the trip had been predetermined, Boncoeur's AutoDrive smoked past the exit.

His destination, Boca Raton, was home to one of the four Mecca's of Computing. Every good programmer, at some point in their lifetime, programmed a computer at one of these U.S. high tech locals. Boca Raton, Florida was home to most of the veteran players who had been in the commercial computer market since day one. IBM, originator of the PC, from which all personal computers could trace their origins, had a corporate campus here as did AMDigital, the descendent of Advanced Micro Devices' merger with a blemished Compaq burdened from the acquisition of Digital. There was Austin, Texas, headquarters to Dell and National Semiconductor, and second only to California's Silicon Valley in the number of baby high tech starter companies. Silicon Valley, land of the American Silicon Entrepreneur and one of the highest divorce rates in the U.S., maintained the greatest in flow of research dollars, an incentive for the minds of Stanford, Berkeley, and Xerox to study.

O'Reilly recalled the look on his son's face as he held the first mouse prototype produced by Xerox's Palo Alto Laboratory in his hand. John smiled as he remembered his son kidding around with him later that day in a San Francisco restaurant, "Dad, the brochure we got at the Palo Alto museum says that mouse was made back in the Seventies. It's as old as you."

Of all four high tech hot spots, O'Reilly knew his way around North Carolina's research triangle the least. He knew Boca the best, which was fine by him since he liked southern Florida the most, especially in December.

The rental car entered IBM's main entrance. He disengaged the automobile's auto pilot. The time was 12:42pm. He was destined for the "Big Boy" building, a nickname given by O'Reilly for two reasons. The edifice held the most satellite dishes on the roof, and standing eight stories, it swelled above all the other buildings on campus. Secondly, some of IBM's biggest computer heads called this place home. They programmed here a minimum from dusk to dawn and did the maximum, seven days a week twenty-four hours a day, more often than not. At least part of the Big Boy was above ground so the coders could see some sunlight a few times a year. O'Reilly had never been in one of Big Boy's underground floors where the really top secret software was written, but he believed the unshackled programmer he had talked with briefly during his last visit. The Big Boy did have a dungeon.

O'Reilly saw two of them standing next to the entrance. They were programmers of the smoking kind. He knew the type well. High strung. Quick tempered. Never wrong and thus always right. If the computer program they wrote didn't work it was the user's problem. If the programmer decided they didn't like the way the program functioned, not that it didn't work in the first place, they would get out the compiler manual, a programmer's bible, to find the answer to the discrepancy. If that didn't do the trick after a couple days of swearing at the manual, they would kick the computer, slightly harder each time. If the computer still booted after the kick that knocked the case off, they would then, and only then, consider asking a fellow human being, a programmer, for assistance. Breaking the machine, the proper programming description for computer, was no big deal. What better way to convince management their hardware was way too slow and they deserved a faster machine anyway which explained why they were behind schedule on the code fix to the bug they, not the user of the program, had discovered?

These were American programmers. A plus. He spoke computer English as they did. O'Reilly tried to mooch a smoke off a Chinese programmer once. All he got for his effort was a pencil already chewed on.

"How's coding in the dungeon these days?"

"You a coder?" the guy with the pack in his hands responded to O'Reilly.

"Yup. I specialize in data warehouses and web frontends. Got a smoke, guy?"

"Sure, man. You know I'm, I mean me and Bert here, writin' front ends to IBM's SNU server. You know what SNU stands for?"

"Something No one Understands," O'Reilly responded which induced an echo of smiles followed by a simultaneous exhalation of smoke from the two IBM programmers. "I did some work on SNU a couple years back. Whoever wrote the API for SNU needs to get their head checked."

"They done checked out of here last year. Now were left empty handed trying to get this stuff to move over to our server code and work right."

"Got a name for it?" as O'Reilly blew.

The Big Blue coders smiled at each other, and said in unison, "SNU II."

One of them looked over O'Reilly in his suit. "You don't dress IBM. You don't dress like a contractor or you'd be wearing everyday clothes like us. Who are ya, man?" said the contractor who looked, and smelled, more like a street bum than an individual with an advanced degree in computer science.

"I'm John O'Reilly of O'Reilly & Associates."

"No shit. Far out man. Aren't you the one who bailed out Nintendo?"

"O'Reilly & Associates did solve a coding problem for Nintendo."

"You need any more programmers? I've got a master's in engineering from California Institute of Technology. I can't take this hired hand shit anymore. You get second class treatment," said the bummin' California programmer.

"I got a B.S. from Georgia Tech, and I got more experience," said the other coder who wasn't too peachy about his working situation either.

O'Reilly gave the two coders a look over. The Caltech coder had holes in his sneakers, but at least he had shoes on. The coder from Georgia was barefoot. Both had holes in their faded blue jeans and stains on their t-shirts. The Caltech programmer's t-shirt had a torn pocket sleeve that flapped in the wind. Only a pen clipped to the other guy's pocket kept it from doing the same. Both were bulging from their shirts, at the belly. They stood the same way they sat in a chair, slouched over. Even their seats had, through years of practice, taken the shape of a chair. The only muscles not atrophied were their wrist muscles due to continual usage of a keyboard. O'Reilly had a better chance of getting a bum off the beach to write computer software the way O'Reilly wanted it written compared to these virtual humans who had become one with the machine.

"I'm out of business cards at the moment."

"That's cool man. What's your web site?"

O'Reilly was trying to loose focus of the smoking software developers. He looked toward Big Boy's entrance as the Georgia tech head babbled from his mind expectations of how things should be at O'Reilly & Associates. He saw the suits. Ten IBM types with blue slacks, white shirts, and a red tie were walking through the door. Ed Rolands, who O'Reilly knew from previous dealings with IBM, was in the pack. O'Reilly moved the hand that held the cigarette to his back as he faced the pack of suits. With the other hand, he waved to Ed who briefly and cautiously smiled back in O'Reilly's direction. Rolands lackluster reception made O'Reilly's cigarette go cold quickly. He did not hesitate to drop the smoke on the ground and give it a quick stomp. None of the pack of suits would openly light up in public though most probably had a carton of cigs in their executive closet. At best, he had shown them he was in control of when to inhale and when to exhale. At worst, he was trying his damnedest to quit.

"It's O'ReillyAssociatessovlecomputerproblems4u.com."

"Is that an english u or a chineese you?" replied the California coder.

"Chinese mathematician who worked for me made that address. I've gotta go guys. Thanks for the smoke."

"I received ya. Cool address, dude," replied the Georgia coder.

The two coders proceeded to debate, argue by non virtual human standards, as to the extent of the computer language knowledge each knew, and, as such, who was the better suited, clean clothes not being a criteria, for the one job O'Reilly had to offer.

Security gave O'Reilly a guest badge. The receptionist directed him to his meeting with IBM's top brass. He was going to the top floor. The doors to the elevator opened to a lobby that looked like the plane he had been in this morning. Surely, he must be on the wrong floor, but an IBM suit approached him and verified he was in the right place. Then the suit gave him an "interview number." The suit was kind enough to point to an electric outlet on the wall, but another suit, non IBM like his, plugged in before he could take his laptop out of his briefcase. Every outlet was in use. He counted the power cords connected to an outlet. Thirty-eight people were plugged in. This was the wrong time to go unplugged. His laptop power meter showed four minutes of battery remaining, barely enough time to boot up Windows 2015.

He was nearly out of power, too. O'Reilly slid in the one empty chair located next to the elevator on its way back down. When he stood up for a seventh inning stretch and a drink of water some suit stole his seat.

He had to ask permission to plug his laptop into a power outlet. The wall clock in the meeting room indicated the time to be 1:02pm. The IBMers were on a tight schedule. He fumbled with his power adapter, inserting and removing the adapter from the laptop. Time and time again the laptop failed to power up. Only after the fourth insertion did he find the culprit. The power adapter was bent out of shape with an indention that matched the last kick he had given to his briefcase in the flying sardine can that got him to the upside down belly of the Big Boy who had just eaten lunch and was getting ready to eat one more sardine, John O'Reilly, for dessert. O'Reilly looked down the long executive table carved from a slab of oak. At the end of the plank sat Captain Blue dressed in his IBM uniform and a marine crew cut. He looked back down the line. All men. All had crew cuts except for two dissimilar suits near Captain Blue. The two suits next to Mr. Blue must belong to the client.

O'Reilly had been in this boat before. The client, as represented by the two suits, had a computer problem. The problem, though created in house, could not be solved by anyone at the company. Whoever wrote the defective program wished they were squatting in the outhouse at the moment. The company couldn't afford to can the programmer because they might figure out what they did wrong and correct the problem on their own. Instead, they would fry the coder. The coder was given a bag of fast food twice a day. As long as the coder gratefully swallowed whatever junk food they forked out, they would keep the coder and even consider giving the poor programmer a cot to sleep on instead of the floor. But they couldn't wait. So the decision was made to hit the panic button and hire another company, IBM, in this case, to fix the problem, which by now had become an emergency because the people in IBM's Big Boy had turned blue trying to fix the problem, too. IBM's role changed from the consultant who could fix the problem to the consultant who could find another consultant capable of fixing the problem. Even if IBM couldn't cool the crisis, they could make money from finding someone who could.

"I've got a faulty power supply, gentlemen. If I could have a computer, it'll take me only a few minutes to swap hard drives and get my presentation underway."

"That won't be necessary, Mr. O'Reilly," responded Captain Blue twenty feet away.

O'Reilly looked at the carpet below comprised of a multitude of blue hues. He'd been cornered in a meeting room full of deadly executives before, but this was the first time he was without his one mean of defense, his laptop computer.

"Mr. O'Reilly, what is your educational background," said a suit to the left of the Big Blue captain.

O'Reilly put his hands behind his back, stood upright, and took a step away from the laptop resting on IBM's table. He looked at the Captain and spoke with no emotion, "I have a Bachelor of Science degree in Computer Science which I earned in 2004 from the University of Missouri at St. Louis."

UMSL which he pronounced to his associates as ' I'm sold, they're not buying if they've got Ivy growing between they're legs.' Not very impressive. This question asked off the bat counted as two strikes.

"Did you graduate with any honors?"

"No."

"Mr. O'Reilly, do you have any background in real-time data authentication using IBM's SecureLink transaction server?"

"No, but I have done," O'Reilly was interrupted by a gentleman sitting at the edge of IBM's wooden ship jostling above the sways and eddies which John O'Reilly now stood upon.

"Thank you for your."

O'Reilly completed his sentence. "I have done extensive work in a variety of secure network environments and I am well versed in over two million forms of communication including ADA, Basic, C, C++, K, D+, Cobol, Fortran, Java, Latte, Smalltalk, Coffeechat, SNU, and recently, SNU II. I'll put IBM's SecureLink protocol on the list. Good day, Gentleman."

With the word 'good' he grabbed his laptop and on the word 'gentleman' he turned his back to walk out of the executive meeting room on the eighth floor of IBM's Fat Boy, the flagship of IBM's armada of campus office buildings. If O'Reilly had a cigarette handy he would have shoved it down the power cord he left behind to light the Big Boy's atomic fuse. Ka Boom. He grinned as he stepped in the elevator. What a waste of his time, and money. This lesson, which he referred to such experiences as, only cost him nine hundred bucks. He had been bent over worse before.

"What are you doing?" Ed Rolands interjected to a table of IBM suits still in the process of digesting the event just transpired.

The 'Thank you for your' suit responded, "He's just another chain smoking coder who got fed up with the company he used to be working for. He can't even plug the power cord into the back of a computer."

"This guy who just had a computer glitch is one of the best break fix programmers in the country! You don't treat someone with fifteen years of coding expertise like he just graduated from college." Ed Rolands stood up as he clinched a fist at the 'Thank you for your' suit.

"He hasn't tackled a problem like this in a couple of years," said another suit.

"He got GM out of one hell of a pinch two years ago," responded Rolands. "I worked with him on an Emerson Electric manufacturing problem last year. He didn't solve it, but neither did anyone else. You just booted a first class businessman out the door."

O'Reilly was walking past the waterfall of IBM's Boca Raton research campus when Ed Rolands caught up with him. O'Reilly didn't hear the first shout Rolands gave some thirty meters away. He ignored the second. O'Reilly turned around to a winded Ed Rolands when he was an arm's length away.

"John, I'm sorry about that."

"I am too, Ed."

"Would you come back and talk. We'll give you the time to make another presentation."

O'Reilly cleared his throat to control the tremble in his voice. "Ed, would you take the time to give a presentation given what occurred?"

Rolands looked at the ground as he swayed his head back and forth. "No, I wouldn't."

"I've got a wife and kids back in St. Louis waiting for me to bring supper home. I still can't get that woman to cook a decent meal for me. Take care, Ed."

"Will you be available this evening?"

O'Reilly grinned a barely perceptible smile. "I always take the business phone home with me."

Rolands smiled, turned around, and walked back to Big Blue. O'Reilly continued his walk to the car. His briefcase swung in a slight arc to and fro, though he still walked as if he were carrying a boat anchor. Ed's words had lightened his load a little.

"Door open." The door to his rental car did not open. This automobile was not equipped with speech recognition. John O'Reilly fumbled for the keys to the car. "Doors," he muttered to himself. Someone locked this door. He did. Every locked door has a key. One just has to find it.

CHAPTER 8

Aloneness is the awareness of one's self. Loneliness is the absence of another.

John awoke at 11am. He had slept ten hours, by his recollection, as 1 am was the last time he remembered looking at the alarm clock. He had fallen asleep with one hand on page 324 of the Computer Shopper Magazine he had bought last night. The other hand he had used as a pillow. He saw this hand as he opened his eyes, yet he could not feel it. His entire right arm was numb. With each rekindling of feeling of each nerve fiber in his right side, he became awake. Today was Sunday, the day of the week he could do as he pleased. He stretched, lifting his arm upward, to lesson the tingle in his arm.

Normally, given a summer day, as today was, he went fishing. If he hurried he could be at his favorite fishing hole by noon. Normally, none of the fish would be biting this time of day. He lifted the blinds to his bedroom window. Not a cloud in the sky. He couldn't pass up such a day with a perfect sky to do some fishing, even if it meant not getting the slightest of a nibble. If the fish were sleeping, he would do a little cat napping, too, upon the lush green grass underneath the spanning limbs of his favorite oak tree.

But something within him did not feel right. The sensation in his arms had subsided to be replaced by a hunger within his stomach. He ate two toaster pastries quickly as he put on an old pair of blue jeans. The yearning within his stomach did not subside. He ate a fruit rollup. Then another. The box was empty. Normally four fruit rollups cured his desire for food. The yearning in his stomach came from another source, a source without substance, which could not be touched. On such a day as today, he would spend the day by himself. He would be alone.

Being under the perfect tree lying upon the perfect grass would provide no cessation to this hunger if there was no other but he to listen to the birds whistle in the air above. His sole breath would provide no reverberation to add to the chorus of birds perched in the tree above. He needed to have another with him. Someone who would enjoy the grass, the tree, the birds, and the fishing as he did.

But who?

Mike, the stocker, was working today at Schnucks. Mark, a computer technician at Best Buy, was spending the day with his girlfriend. Jovita? No. Jovita wouldn't want to go fishing with him. John looked at his hand. Two of his fingers were still numb. He didn't need these fingers to count the number of people he considered to be his friend. But this need, the need to remove loneliness, had to be amputated, to be removed from his self.

What about the old man he helped out last night?

Maybe he needed a friend. Maybe he would go fishing with him today. Did the old man like him? Not at the grocery store, but he seemed amicable enough at the dumpster. Did the old man like fishing? John needed to find out.

There was only one problem. Where did the old man live?

John always put his trash in the garbage bin closest to his apartment door, the same garbage bin he helped the old man last night. People who dwelt in his apartment building 14452 and those who made apartment building 14448 their home would find this dumpster to be the closest. This meant if he were to knock on the sixteen doors to the apartments in 14452 and the sixteen doors in 14448 and all the residents were in their apartment and each resident opened their door when he knocked he would find the old man. John found no reassurance in this thought. He'd never even knocked on the eight doors on the east half of 14452, of which one was his. Maybe he would find the old man outside, which was possible, given such a day as today.

He opened the patio sliding glass door blinds to get a full view of the sky above. The intensity of the Sun's illumination was so great he was forced to squint. The light shined in and gave his one bedroom, one bath, one living and dining room area apartment color. A single lamp in his bedroom dimmed in comparison. Every inch of his 650 square foot apartment was exposed to the Sun's rays.

He had three pieces of furniture. A single upholstered reclining chair sat near the doorway. A table and an old wooden chair occupied some space near the kitchenette. Against the opposite wall from the chair was a row of books. The books, about twenty in all, were on the floor. The floor served as a bookshelf and a desk. Another five books in the middle of the living room were opened and arranged in a semicircle so all could be read, and touched, at the same time.

John did not have a color television. He did have a 13-inch black and white TV on the table next to the kitchenette. Next to the TV was an old FM/AM radio with a single antenna pointed straight up. A piece of aluminum foil linked this antenna to the TV's rabbit ear. The other ear was missing. John did not have cable. He strained his vision to watch four channels, ABC, CBS, KPLR, and PBS, as he put one finger on the aluminum foil to improve reception. In order to watch PBS he had to use both hands, one on the antenna and the other tapping the volume control. Why it worked he did not know, but it worked.

The outside light lessened the dreariness of the barren walls of his apartment. He was absorbed by the Sun's rays and the grandeur of the day as he looked outside from behind his patio sliding glass door. His eyes adjusted to the light. First, he could discern a slab of concrete, his patio, directly in front of him. Others in the apartment complex had lawn furniture, maybe even a gas grill. He had neither. His patio was bare except for a small rusty metal garbage can left near the dumpster by someone. John recycled this bucket, using it to hold aluminum cans and bottles he found scattered throughout the Country Club's parking lot. He picked up these items on his walk home from Schnucks, getting a few extra dollars in the process.

The walkway leading from the parking lot to his apartment building came into view, followed by a flat expanse. He could see green. The lawn, with dimensions sixty yards by thirty yards, was a sea of Bermuda grass with a clump of crabgrass here and there. The expanse was faced by three apartment buildings, one of which was his, 14452. To his left was an apartment building whose inhabitants would not use the trash dumpster where he met the old man last night.

Apartment building 14448, on the other side of the lawn, faced his patio window. He looked at this apartment building closely, in particular, at the patio directly opposite his. He could see lawn furniture, a white table with a red and white umbrella in the center to shelter the table and four chairs from the Sun's radiation. On the umbrella was the Budweiser logo, the same logo in neon lights in the window of the Country Club.

Too easy. This was too easy. Lying on the patio was a bottle tipped on its side. From this distance he could not read the label; however, the bottle on the patio was very similar in shape to the bottles he had fetched for the old man last night.

Did the old man live in this apartment?

If he was going to do this he had to do it now. The day was getting too old to go fishing. He opened the patio sliding glass door. The emptiness in his stomach was filled with another sensation, the fluttering of butterflies, churning his hunger for a friend into the anxiety of not finding a friend. He hadn't taken his anti depressant pill this morning. He could do it if he swallowed his Prozac. Rather than chase it with a chug from a gallon milk jug, he elected to swallow it dry as he walked across the lawn. John gulped when he was halfway to the patio with the Budweiser lawn furniture. His gait was slow until the bottles came in clear view. A bottle of Glen Livet. He galloped the rest of the distance to the old man's apartment.

But what if someone else, beside the old man, had drunk this particular Glen Livet bottle? What if the old man had drank on the lawn last night and someone in this apartment had picked up the bottle? Maybe the old man didn't live here. Maybe he was visiting the person who lived in this apartment. John's walk slowed to a crawl.

The wheel in John's head spun. What could he do without knocking on the door to find out if the old man lived here? What he could is check the names on the mailboxes next to the entrance of the apartment building! He opened the apartment building entrance door, immediately to the left of the Budweiser lawn furniture. The mailboxes for all residents were on the right wall of the entrance hallway, identical to his apartment building, except the mailboxes were on the left wall as one entered his building, 14448.

No one was in the hallway. He breathed with relief. No one would ask what he was doing looking at the names on mailboxes. What was the old man's name? He couldn't remember. He thought about the day before. Had the man said his name? No. Anxiety brewed in John's stomach. As he reopened the entrance door the anxiety in his belly was replaced with emptiness. He stood in the doorway, with the door halfway open, and from this mixture of anxiety and emptiness stirred a new feeling in his gut. Of the 190 pounds in his body he had produced an ounce of courage. He was going to find out if the man lived here.

He tapped on the door gently once. What would he say?

He muttered to himself, "Hi, I helped you get your bottles out of the trash last night. I'm going to the lake to do some fishing. Want to come along?"

No. Stupid. The old man knew who he was. Dumb. Other than the three rivers, Meramac, Missouri, and Mississippi, lakes were the only bodies of water nearby to go fishing. Of course, one would go to the lake. No one fished on the Mississippi nowadays.

He knocked again, slightly louder, but surely too softly to disturb anyone inside. No sooner had John knocked the second time did the door open. Before him stood the old man with one hand holding an ice pack to his forehead. In the other hand was a nearly empty whiskey bottle.

"Ya, wanda want, kid?"

John stuttered. He looked down at the man's feet. The man was wearing slippers with bunnies on the ends. From the calves down the man's legs were cleanly shaven. From the calf up they were very, very hairy up to his mid thigh, which at this juncture was covered by a silk robe pink in color with frilly lace. The robe was certainly not made for a man, being entirely too short, but suited a woman well. John looked up and tried again.

"I don't have all day, kid." The man looked John directly in the face. "Ya gotta a mouth, use it."

John blurted out the words in his mind, "Want to go fishing?"

"Go fishin' with you? Why I diddant think ya had it in ya."

"I go fishing all the time. Always bring back some good catch. Should be easy pickings today. I know a good watering hole, but we've got to hurry or we won't get any bites, just nibbles."

"Well, I be. I done got ya figured wrong, kid. You young whippersnapper, you. You kids. Why back in my hay day we didn't go fishin' till mid afternoon at the earliest." The old man smiled as he took a swig from his bottle.

John wondered why one would wait till almost sundown to go fishing. Maybe the old man liked to fish for carp.

"You're not gonna get any then except some mud scrapers. Not very tasty. Mid afternoon is way too late to get started. Want to go now?"

John gave a shaky nod. The old man definitely wanted to do some fishing today. He almost had him convinced. John continued.

"I've got all the equipment. All you need to do is put on your fishing clothes. Don't need a hat. We'll be sitting in the shade reeling 'em in right and left. Even got an extra pole for you."

The old man laughed, "You kids, nowadays are so wild and crazy. I got my own pole. I always keep it handy to do some fishin'. Ya never know when ya might putit to use. Haven't been able to get it stiff lately, but I can still hold it up most of the time, even if I can't get it up. You all right, kid. This old man sur needs to do some fishin' with a young whiphersnaper likeya."

"Then you'll go fishing with me?"

"Of course, I'll go fishin' with ya. Give me a few to getin my huntin' gear."

The old man spread his arms wide to give him a look of grandeur, and in doing so exposed some very hairy armpits to the young lad.

"As surely, as the Sun never set on the British Empire a hundred years ago, I am always a willing participant in the great art of chasing those fine slippery things which us men simply refer to as 'going fishin'."

John didn't understand the last statement. He was still pondering his confusion resulting from the words, 'haven't been able to get my pole stiff lately.' Maybe the old man was a fly fisherman. Those poles have a lot of bend to them. John was in complete elation in obtaining a fishing friend. He said to the man before the apartment door closed, "I've done some fly fishing!"

"I always let my fly loose 'fore I do my fishin'. Howdaya kids gets to be so kinky? Can't wait to find out. See ya in a few."

John pondered this statement as he walked across the lawn to his apartment. His remark about kids being wild and crazy seemed strange. What did this have to do with fishing? John smirked. Maybe the old man was slightly senile. Nonetheless, he had made a new friend. He was going fishing with someone.

John grabbed the tackle box in his apartment. His fishing poles were already in his pickup truck. He always left the poles in his pickup bed. Even though someone could easily take them, no one ever did. He had nine poles. Most were a little rusty from being exposed to the elements continuously, but still served their purpose well. How about showing up at the old man's door with a couple of cane poles, one in each hand? What better way to get the old man hooked on the idea of spending the rest of the day reeling in some fresh fish?

John knocked on the door with some excitement. He stood at the old man's doorway with complete confidence. He pounded on the door again.

"Give me a second, kid. I don't hustle like I used to. Gotta get these damn drawers zipped up!" yelled the old man from within the confines of his apartment.

John stood a solid minute at attention anxiously awaiting the old man's appearance. He couldn't wait any longer. It was time to go fishing. The day was aging. He reached his hand out to put his hand on the door. The door opened.

Before him stood the old man. His bunny slippers had been replaced with suede shoes. His legs were covered with skin tight black leather pants, which bulged at the midsection. His shirt, like the robe, was made of silk. The shirt was only partially buttoned exposing his chest nearly down to the belly button. His chest was very, very hairy, the hair being solid black, matching the shade of shirt exactly. Indeed, if one did not pay close attention, the man could claim not to be wearing any shirt at all or wearing a shirt buttoned up to the neck. But what was on the man's very hairy chest stood out the most. Not one, not two, not three, but at least four solid gold chains of varying lengths. Had John desired to sift through the old man's chest hair, he could have found a few more strands of gold. John looked at the man's arms. They were cleanly shaven. On one arm, at the wrist, was an expensive gold watch, perhaps a Rolex. On the man's fingers were more bands of gold. Some fingers had more than one ring. The one on his right pinky caught John's onlooking stare for the greatest length of time. The pinky ring was misshapen, appearing to be a warped wedding ring, for on one obtuse end jutting an inch above the man's extremity was a huge diamond ring. John took it all in. This was very odd fishing attire, better suited for the manager of a professional wrestler. John's mouth was open. He was aghast.

The old man looked at the boy dressed in overalls and holding two cane fishing poles, one in each hand. "What the fuck is going on here, Opie?"

John became tense. He spoke nervously. "Do you want to go fishing dressed like that?"

"What the hell! Listen Opie Taylor when you said fishin', I thought ya meant fishin' fishin'. I ain't gonna go fishin' with ya boy. That's duller than watching the Stars and Stripes Banner fuckling spankin' and wavin' on PBS before it done shut down for the night."

The boy dropped one pole as he held onto the other pole to support himself. His face trembled as he tried to contain the tears welling in his eyes. He looked down at the dropped pole.

"Get lost! Go play with your daddy, boy!"

As John O'Reilly walked off the old man opened the patio blinds to his apartment to watch the boy limp home, using the two poles as crutches. He took a swig from a new bottle of Glen Livet scotch.

"What the hell did the world do to you, boy?"

The world did not do anything else to John O'Reilly that day. He sat in his bed, unable to sleep, unable to cry, only to stare out the window and gaze at a cloudless day become another dreamless dark night.

CHAPTER 9

The stewardess offered to give a broken businessman a ride for free. His wife wanted to fix him permanently.

The plane left Miami bound for St. Louis on schedule. Not that it mattered. He had plenty of time to board his 3:50pm flight. Plenty of time to sit around in the airport lounge and mope about his situation. Even a couple of cigarettes and a Jack Daniel shot of hard whiskey didn't change his view on this so called life of his and what a meager existence it amounted to.

"Marketing. It was all marketing," he told some poor soul who had happened to sit in an empty chair next to his seat of doom and despair. John O'Reilly limped to the plane. The first person to check in at the gate, and the last to board the plane.

He heaved a sigh of relief to sit down in a plane that was nearly empty. The laptop. Now all he had to do was get up and sling that boat anchor in an overhead storage bin. He tried once. Twice. Not yet. He sighed again and again and again. His cheeks stretched and sunk pulsating to a sullen rhythm like his mouth were the blowhole of a beached blue whale. The hell with it. The hell with his soon to be bankrupt business.

His legs were too heavy to stand up. Why not leave the laptop in the chair beside him? He'd program it to say, "I understand how you feel," to his every statement. He gave a slight laugh between sighs. He'd say back, " And I understand how you feel about sitting in that damned chair next to me. That's why you're broke." Then he smiled with complete cynicism. "Good luck on trying to find a battery unit for a two year old laptop."

He began to stroke the case of the laptop. "My poor trusty faithful. You've come through in the clutch time and time again. Now you're going to that great parts storage center in my basement, but you're data will live on with the big data chief upstairs, forever. Our relationship has come to and end, my dented Fingermate."

"I understand how you feel."

John turned his head. Someone was behind him. She was attractive, mid twenties, and had nice white teeth. He could tell because she was giving him a photo shot smile. He tried his best to smile back. He'd seen her face before. She was the same stewardess who had given him award winning service on his trip to Boca, home of the Big Boy who was probably doing a few burps right now from all the businessmen he had chewed on today. O'Reilly hoped the Big Boy suffered from worse indigestion than he this evening.

"Huh?" replied O'Reilly.

"I called it off yesterday with my fiancée, Hal. My relationship with him has just come to an end, too," the stewardess replied with a look of sorrow to match the sunken face of the broken down businessman sitting down in a slump.

"Well actually, I've been married for sixteen years. She doesn't want to cook for me, but," John O'Reilly was interrupted with another exquisite smile from the stewardess.

"Would you like to sit up front in the first class section, we've got plenty of space?"

"Yes." The thought of reclining fully gave him the boost he needed to get out of his seat designed for a child. He had enough energy to make the trek to a big person chair.

He followed the stewardess to the first class seating. He looked at her. What a nice seat she had. He watched her walk. Her hips swung. He didn't remember her walking this way this morning. She turned around.

"My name's Kerstin."

"I'm John."

"Well, here we are John, just where a man like you needs to take a load off your feet, in the first class business seating."

"Thanks Kerstin. You've been very generous. I'm sure you'll get an award for your service."

She smiled with a giggle. She lifted her shoulders just like a little girl would who had just received a Popsicle from the ice cream man.

"You're not at all like the other businessmen flying to and from St. Louis. We're not too busy. I could go ahead and get you something to eat, now, if you'd like, and a free drink, too?"

"I can't. My stomach is still churning from a sour business meeting I had a few hours back in Boca Raton."

"What's your business?"

"I'm a consultant. I solve computing problems for corporations. I'm what's called in the business a break-fix man. You know how plumbers can charge anything they want when the pipes get clogged in your house?"

"Ya."

"Well, I'm sort of like a plumber for the computer industry. I get the crap out of computers that keeps them from working."

"Really? That's interesting." She smiled.

John needed a boost to his self image. He needed to inflate his ego. "And when I do fix a problem for a Fortune 500 company, I can charge them any price I want for my services. I brought home over half a million two years ago. Not that that was enough for my wife."

When he said half a million the stewardess put her body within half a foot of the businessman. The broken businessman got a close up of a bosom that could bust a marriage in a heartbeat.

"So why is this plane as filled, I mean, empty anyway?"

"The tourist don't fill up the afternoon flight for some reason. The 9 o'clock flight into Miami from St. Louis hasn't been busy either."

John O'Reilly grinned back to her. "That figures," he said to himself. He shook his head in disagreement at the money he had blown away today. But had he flown with better service than this?

"Hmmm," her eyebrows lifted in inquisition.

"Oh, nothing. I just hope my wife will be at the airport to pick me up."

"I live in St. Louis. Do you need a ride?" She put her hand on John O'Reilly's shoulder. "Will your wife be there for you?"

This was definitely more than award winning service. Must be the tailor made suit he had on. His wife said he looked good in it. He looked at the wedding ring on his finger.

"I've got to call my wife, Kerstin."

The stewardess slowly slid her hand off of the businessman's shoulder. "Sure, I understand."

He picked up his phone and hit auto dial button one, the number he called most frequently, his wife's office at her vet hospital. No answer just voice mail. On the sixth time of hitting the auto dial button, his wife answered.

"Hi John. How was it?"

"Lousy. Complete waste. Laptop didn't survive the day. But I think the plane is on time. Would you be at the airport? I don't feel like waiting around."

"I can't honey. I'm running behind. I've still got the Grisshom's three dogs and the King's cat to look at. Are you sure your plane is on time?"

"Hold on, let me ask Kerstin."

"Who's Kerstin?"

"The stewardess, honey," John said emphasizing the word 'honey.'

"John O'Reilly why do you know the stewardess on a first name basis?"

"She offered to let me sit in one of the big seats for free."

The voice on the phone had been in control, but quickly lost all control. "John, what the hell have you been up to in that airplane!"

"Nothing. She just wanted to get dinner for me, that's all. And something to drink."

"Have you been drinkin' on that plane!"

"Nope. I drank on the airport."

"How much!"

"I just hung out with my good friend, Jack Daniels, for a couple of hours."

"Are you drunk!"

"I don't think so."

"You better behave yourself! I'll be at the airport to pick you up."

"OK." Good. Maybe this time his wife would be at the terminal to pick him up on time. He smiled at Kerstin as she gave him a pillow to rest his weary head. He had a boyish grin on his face as he napped. The trip would be a total success if his wife would be at the airport to greet him. She was never at the airport to greet him on time. Maybe this time she would, and with this thought he slept like a baby in a cradle meant for kings.

"John. John." O'Reilly opened one eye half way. "Ya, honey. I'll drive you home. I'm awake. I'll drive careful this time. I promise." Someone giggled. The voice was not his wife's. He opened both eyes.

"You poor overworked businessman, you. John, you need to sit up all the way. We're about to land."

He stretched. "Thanks Kerstin."

The plane landed. He looked out the window to see if he could spy his wife standing next to the large glass windows of the terminal gate. She wasn't there. He stepped off the plane hoping to see his wife standing there. She wasn't there. He walked out the gate towards the main corridor of Lambert International's east wing. He swayed as he swung his briefcase like it was a crate full of rotten melons. He didn't look up but from the multitude of feet about him he could tell the airport was busy.

Woops. He looked up to avoid another tired traveler. He smiled. Thirty yards down the corridor was his wife, and standing next to her a surprise. Mrs. O'Reilly had brought his little girl. They were looking back at him, but neither gave any indication of his presence. His wife was saying something to Kathy and making some strange arm movements.

"Ok, Kathy, you've seen All in the Family haven't you?"

"I did one time Mommy but I like Sesame Street better."

"Well, do you remember how Edith Bunker would run from the kitchen when Archie called her?"

"Like the cookie monster when he wanted a cookie?"

"Just follow Mommy and walk the way she does." Mrs. O'Reilly sprang into a fast jog of very short steps. She extended her arms to embrace her husband twenty yards away. Her heels clanged barely clinging to her feet and her head bobbed just like the doll with a broken neck Kathy held in her hand.

John O'Reilly stared at the two true to life Barbie dolls, one big, one small, running towards him. He opened his arms to receive them, and as he did so he could see Kerstin, the stewardess who broke it off with her fiancée, stroll by yanking her luggage behind her.

John kissed his wife.

"Daddy, kiss me, too!" and so John O'Reilly lifted his little girl into his arms and kissed her, too. He was home.

The ride to the house was quiet. Kathy O'Reilly got the conversation going. She wanted to know all about Boca Raton and where it was on the map in Florida. She wanted to know how planes fly much faster than cars. She wanted to know why Mommy had only said a few sentences on the way to the airport. She wanted to know if Daddy had made a new friend on the airplane. John O'Reilly answered the first two with flying colors. The last two questions he elected to go back and answer the first two questions in more detail. As Mrs. O'Reilly parked the car in the two car garage of the O'Reilly residence, each O'Reilly could hear the brakes of the Cavalier squeak.

Kathy got out of the car with her legs rolling down the runway and her arms spread like wings. John lugged his broken laptop followed closely by Mrs. O'Reilly. All three O'Reilly's could hear Mrs. O"Reilly close the driver door to the Cavalier. Mr. O'Reilly nearly dropped his briefcase. Kathy nearly collided with the garage wall, opening the entrance to the house barely in time. Each O'Reilly went their separate way. Mr. O'Reilly elected to go straight to the closet. He thought it was a wise decision to take his time changing clothes this evening.

He needed to smoke. He closed the closet door. He sat down on the small stool next to his closet refrigerator reserved for such occasions. The closet door opened very slowly. It creaked. Before him stood the imposing figure of his wife. In her hand was the belt she had worn today, but now closely resembled a noose. He inhaled one more time from the cigarette. This would be his last smoke tonight.

"You told me you where going to quit smoking," Mrs. O'Reilly said calmly.

"I'm trying. I've only had five today, and it's been a rather hectic day."

"You need to try a little harder, John. You promised me." She paused. "Who was she?"

John put a stupid face on. "Who was who?"

"Don't give me that stupid look! That stewardess was eyeing you when you got off the plane."

John put on a 'happy I'm successful' face. " She just wanted to look at a handsome man in an expensive business suit."

"Take that conceited look off your face!"

John frowned. His wife knew all of his faces. He had one face left. His best one. The frown he took to a grimace followed by a look of anxiety. Then he hit her with his best draw, his angelic, 'I can do no wrongdoing because I'm a boy scout' face. Now it was time to plead the fifth.

"I'm not saying anything, because anything I say you'll use against me because you think I've been up to no good." John paused. His brow shifted to a hint of anger. "There is nothing for me to say because you know I love you."

"Don't you sweet talk to me!" A moment later the last sentence John O'Reilly spoke registered in Mrs. O'Reilly's mind. She mellowed. You were flirting with that girl weren't you?"

"Look. I was trying to stuff my laptop in a sardine this morning. She offered to help. I played along even though she

61

couldn't stuff anymore. I looked at her stuffing but I'm tired and I'm hungry enough to eat any food you'll cook me."

Mrs. O'Reilly countenance turned to complete confusion. Mr. O'Reilly bolted for the door to the closet, striding carefully past his stunned senorita for the kitchen. His daughter was coloring at the kitchen table. John sat beside her and started to critique her art work. He was safe. He positioned himself at the table so his daughter was between him and the entrance to the kitchen. His wife entered the kitchen. She was still in her business suit.

Kathy stopped coloring to look up at her Mom. "Mommy, me and Daddy are hungry. Are you going to make us something to eat?"

"You tell your Father I'll make him something to eat when he tells me what happened on that airplane."

"I did nothing wrong on that airplane!"

The O'Reilly's daughter started to cry. Between sobs, she blurted out the words, " Mommy and Daddy are going to break up and get divorced just like Katy's Mommy and Daddy."

Both of Kathy's parents came to their daughter's aid. John held his daughter's right hand. His wife held Kathy's left hand.

"Daddy's not going to divorce your Mom."

Kathy's crying eased. Mrs. O'Reilly softly stroked her child's arm. "Mommy's not going divorce Daddy unless he trades me in for a newer model of Mommy."

Kathy started to cry again.

"Oh come on. That's enough. I've been driving the same car for sixteen years. What makes you think I'm going to trade you in?" John looked his wife square in the face.

Kathy looked at her Dad. She was confused.

"Kathy." Kathy, with a look of lingering agitation, gazed back at her Mother. "What would make you feel better?"

Kathy smiled. "I want to see the Ward and June Show."

"The Ward and June Show will make you happy?"

Kathy looked at her Mom, then her Dad, and nodded in affirmation.

"Then the Ward and June Show it is. Ward, go get your business suit back on. I'll put my heels on. I think I know where my pearl necklace is and, yes, I know where my matching bracelet is. Kathy go get your best dressed Barbie doll."

The O'Reilly's started to break away the kitchen table, but were interrupted by a loud thumping. Someone was running up the stairs from the basement. John O'Reilly looked at his son as he entered the kitchen. Mrs. O'Reilly did the same. The boy did not look back. He went directly to the refrigerator and opened the door. He stuck his face in the fridge. The rest of the O'Reilly's could hear the fridge's shelves rattle and the lids open and close.

"Mom, there's nothing to eat!" said the boy from behind the refrigerator door. He peered from over the refrigerator door. His hair was dark black. He stood up and closed the fridge door. He was almost six feet tall. He was thin. Lanky would be a better description. An extra twenty pounds in the arms and legs would be needed before the facial hair stubble he had would be called a man's beard not shaved for a day. He had some acne, but the pimples were not numerous and not severe. He was the spitting image of his father when John O'Reilly was fifteen years younger. With a few more years, the boy's acne would subside, his beard would become fuller, his arms and legs would thicken, his shoulders would become broader, and his eyes would be able to just look over a bald man standing six feet tall. In a few years, John Jr. would look exactly like his father.

"John Jr. were putting on an episode of the Ward and June Show. Do you want to help us out, and whistle the tune to Leave It to Beaver for us?"

The teenager looked at his Mom, "You guys are weird."

CHAPTER 10

It took some hard work from Don but he got the weekend rolling.

Donald Murphy, the old man who didn't pay for munched on donuts at the supermarket, tried to grab the entrance door to the clubhouse of Village Green apartments once. He tried to push in on the door a couple of times. He pounded on the window to the manager's office more than a few times.

A lady in her mid forties sat behind the desk in the manager's office. She was fumbling through the desk drawers searching for a set of keys. That someone was pounding on the glass window ten feet away from her was obvious. She ignored the noise. A cigarette was burning in an ashtray on the desk. She reached up to inhale, and in so doing caught a glimpse of Don standing at the window. He pounded on the glass. She went back to searching through her desk.

"Let me in. Let me in. Denise I see you. I see you. I see ya." The middle aged office manager of Village Green apartments looked up again when she heard her name. He puckered up on the word 'you' and shot her several kisses, ones just like a lesser species of primates, a chimpanzee, would make.

"I'll be your handy man, you're candy man, and your lovey dovey man if you want me to. I'll be your primate of love. I know you want me to."

She motioned with her arms to go to the entrance door.

"It's locked. I'm locked from your love. I need it so. I need it 'cause I know you need me so. I need you to unlock the door to your love. I need it so 'cause I know ya need me so, toooey." He sneezed, using his hand as a make shift handkerchief.

Denise Johnson walked to the entrance of the clubhouse. Don Murphy met her at the door. He pushed in on the door. Denise, in turn, pushed on the door.

"Don, it wasn't locked." She shook her head. "You're a sixty year old man and you can't figure out how to open up the door to the Village Green Apartments clubhouse?"

"I knew how to open the door to your heart. I just wanted you to open it up for me."

"This is the door to the leasing office and clubhouse." She shook her head again, this time with a smile. "I don't think I'll ever understand you."

"Good." Don walked through the door. "Keep ya on your toes that way. Frankly, I don't know how I do it myself. It's a secret even to my own mind." He gave her a Sean Connery 007 stare. " I'm your agent of love." He reached into his trousers. "Just give me a second to find my gun. I can't whip it out like I used to."

"Would you quit it! I can't find the keys to the closet having all the recreational stuff. I'm busy. I don't have time for your shenanigans now." Denise, a thin lady with a somewhat elderly gait, made it back to the desk.

The old man stood up from his shooting position. He followed her. He replaced the suave debonair stare with a sincere 'I've never chopped down a cherry tree' grin.'

"Listen, I was just trying to put a smiley face on ya, that's all."

The blemishes of anger covering her face vanished. She shined a smile with a youthful glow, a glow that Athena, the Greed goddess, with all her wisdom would radiate. " What do you want, Don?"

"Well, if you must know, my bath water is cold."

"Must be the water heater. I'll get someone out there on Tuesday." The office manger took out her apartment repair logbook and started to write an entry.

"Tuesday? It's Saturday. Two days without any hot water?" said Don with a hue of blue ice upon his cheeks, a look of frigid hopelessness.

"It's Labor Day weekend. The maintenance crew is off on Monday."

Don pretended to turn the cold knob on the faucet wide open. He shivered. He tried to sneeze.

"OK. I'll try to send someone to your apartment today."

"Thank you, Denise. You're a lifesaver, and sweet as one, too. Uh, Uh."

"What else?" She liked his sweet statement.

"The garbage disposal is stopped up."

"How did it get clogged, Donald?"

Donald whimpered, " That maid of mine cooks my roast so brick stiff not even the garbage disposal can get it down. Now all it does is make a rattlin' tin tin tin noise."

"I beg your pardon. Mr. Murphy, who are you calling maid of mine?"

Don replied with a sneeze not completely contained by his cupped hands.

Watching the old man helplessly hold jaundice colored mucous as it began to ooze through his fingers softened her demeanor.

"Donald, did you check to see if maybe your silverware got put in the disposal somehow?"

"I'm not checking down there. That's disgusting. I'm not gonna grab stiff meat. That's gross."

"But you'll reach into your trousers?" She handed him a Kleenex.

He smirked as he wiped. "I'm an old man. Why you want make fun of an old man with meat problems."

She continued to write. She tried not to smile. "I'll get someone to look at the sink, too."

"Uh, one other thing."

"You're pushing it, Don. What now?"

"The refrigerator light doesn't turn off. That miniature guy who does light bulb control done quit turning the lights off."

She tried to refrain from laughing by smiling profusely and feigning a hiccup. "How do you know that? Don't tell me you're climbing into the fridge and closing the door."

"Denise, that's crazy. I knoze the light doesn't turn off."

She closed her eyes to control a single tear of laughter, and as she wiped her eyes she said," How do you know?"

"My whiskey taste don't taste like it used to."

"What! Donald Murphy your not suppose to be drinkin'. That's not what you're doctor told you to be doing!"

"What the doctor says. What the doctor says. What the doctor says. What the doctor said and I quote, 'If you stop drinkin', you'll lighten your load.' Well, my load is sitting in the fridge all lit up all the time."

"Good. Maybe you won't age so fast if you keep you're scotch from aging more in the fridge."

"He wasn't right about the drinkin' part. My malt liquor taste even better! I've discovered an improved distillation process. I'm writin' to the patent office tomorrow. I can't believe I didn't discover this years ago."

"Donald Murphy you're unbelievable!"

"I know. I can't believe I got to be so great myself."

"Don, the doctor said you've got to stop drinking."

"I'm tryin'. I'm tryin'. I'm tryin'. How am I going to quit if my whiskey gots a new flavor. I need to go back to drinkin' that old dull taste I'm so used to." He paused. He needed. "Do ya think maybe you could get me 'nother batch. I won't drink it so fast this time. I promise."

"You promised me when you moved here you wouldn't drink at all."

"It was the light bulb guy, Denise. He's been drinkin' most of my booze. Not all of it, I admit I drunk at least a little."

"Don, you're not funny anymore." She gave him a cold stare. " I'm letting you live here rent free. I give you treatment better than I give my best residents, and you repay me by asking me to fill up your fridge."

Don removed his entertainment mask. He leaned over the desk and spoke softly with a somber face to the office manager. "Denise, I'm old. I'm happy when I'm drunk. Let me be happy."

The office manager tried to hold back a tear. She could not. "The doctor said if you'd quit drinking and take care of yourself." She paused. "He said maybe you'd get."

Don interrupted. "Doc said maybe, not big maybe, but tiny weenie maybe. I think maybe what I need to do is have a few more hurrahs, while I still got it in me. Don put on a cheerful smile. Time for a different subject. "So what's the deal with all the kids standin' around outside next to the pool anyway?"

"I can't get our fifth annual Village Green residents Labor Day Weekend pool get together wound up. They're not even drinking from a keg of free beer. I'm going to have leftover beer this year."

Don grinned like a cat in front of the door to a birdcage left wide open. "Don't even ask. The only leftovers you're getting are the weenies."

"I'd rather be winding down in the nursing home, too, if I'd have to go to what you just described as a dead party."

She scowled. "Mr. Hot Dog, you have a Ph.D. in Partying. Why don't you earn your keep and help me get this thing going."

The old man felt he had the upper hand. "What are you going to do for me?"

"Don't you even try! You get your behind out there now and get to work while I go get the water volleyball net and beach ball. And I better not see you samplin' the booze."

Don lifted his paws to his face. He shook his rear end. He stuck his tongue out and looked at the manager with hungry and downtrodden eyes. "I can have a piece of a burger can't I?"

She laughed. "Get out there you goofball and make those kiddies giggle."

Don walked straight to the beer keg. "Excuse me. Hey you. Ya you, man. Pour me some beer while it's still cold." The young man poured. "Thanks guy, you've saved me from dehydration." Don drank as the boys and girls mulling around the beer keg watched.

"Don't stop pouring, dude."

"You've got a full cup," replied the muscular man with a thick chest and arms as large as his legs.

"The other glass, guy." Don waived another plastic cup in the muscle head's face. "This way I won't have to ask ya to pour again, allright? What's your name anyway?"

The man replied very simply and somewhat sternly, "Joe."

"As in Joe Camel?" retorted old Don.

"No, as in Joe Barnes." The muscle head could give no better response. The strong man with a weak head filled the cup.

Don lifted both cups, alternating a drink from each. "Look, I'm lifting. I'm weightlifting. I might be old, but I can still do sixteen ounces at a time."

The muscle man roared in laughter, the only rebuke he could think of invoking. The girls around him giggled at Don in unison.

A young lady with porcelain white skin and with a mind not in the toilet wasn't humored by Don's busy hands. She was also unhappy the muscle man was paying the least attention to her from the assortment of bikini babes about him. She retorted, "There's nothing funny about drinking two beers at once."

"Listen up. I go into the Country Club next door everyday. I always get three beers all at once when I sit at the bar. The bartender asked me a month ago why I do this. I say to him, 'I've got two distant brothers over in Ireland, and the two extra beers I drink every evenin' for them. And they told me they over there drinkin' three at a time to remember me, too. This way, even though we apart we drink together."

Some of the crowd laughed slightly. Others did not.

Don's voice changed. He spoke with an unmistakable Irish accent. "Well yesterday I went to the bar and only got two beers. Bartender said, 'What's up?' I told him my doctor told me to quit drinkin'. So that's why I only got two beers just now." Everyone laughed. Even the girl who didn't want to worship the sewer king unclogged her windpipe.

Mr. Murphy could see the office manger walking toward the enclosed pool area with a net. She dropped the deflated beach ball. The old man had most of the girl's and boy's attention at the pool party, and in the process they stopped moping to music that once had a beat with barely a pulse. Now the music was hopping. Grandpa Murphy further amplified the sound by jumping a little jig. The kiddies gathered around him quickly picked up the rhythm of his dance. Dancing Donald stopped. He was winded but he still had a laugh in him.

"I went out on a date yesterday. She was almost as old as me." Don looked at one of the bikini babes. "But she was almost as cute as you. Anyway, we're rolling around on the couch and one thingy, even you know what I mean by thingy, leads to another. We're old, but we still gotta enough left to make it to bed." He breathed. "Afterwards, if you know what I mean by afterwards, I say to her, 'Denise, I pretty sure that's what she told me her name was. If I knew ya were a virgin I woulda waited till the second date.' She says back to me, 'Don, if I would have known you could still make your thingy get a stiffy, I would have taken my pantyhose off!'"

Everyone in the pool area laughed. Some of the kids, caught gulping when Don threw the punch line, were spitting mouthfuls of beer on the cement. Most had a hard time holding onto their plastic cup. The beer spilled from their cups in response to the vibration of cheer spewing forth from their bodies. One young man dropped his container altogether.

Don looked at the young man, at most a couple years short of twenty. "We need to get ya a cup with one of those lids on top of it." The sixteen-year old looked back. "When the office manager gets ya one, tell her I need one, too. I'm just like you. I can't hold my cup, either. Not like I used to."

The boy nodded.

"By the way, kid, who does your diapers? 'Cause I'm overdue for a diaper washin'. My maid won't take care of 'em for me." Don pointed at Denise.

The office manager, with the deflated beach ball under her right arm and the net draped over her right shoulder closed the gate to the pool area with her other hand. Don waived to her. He grinned. He stretched his grin some more with a pull of his unshaven whiskers. A cat hiding a mouthful of feathers behind exposed teeth couldn't have grinned wider.

Everyone around Don snickered at the Village Green Apartments office manager in a similar subdued fashion. They were all thinking of a thought. One that, innately they conceived, should not be openly expressed.

Denise walked around the pool next to the keg of beer where Don was standing. "What did you say to these kids? They're looking at me, with a look, like they know something they shouldn't know."

"I didn't say nothing you wouldn't be proud of, besides, the cement around the pool finally got wet. You told me to get these kids soakin' in laughter. How am I gonna do it, if I don't make an entrée with a splash?"

Denise didn't respond.

"Ya know, the only way to get these Midwestern daughters and corn boys wet is to show 'em the way. Hey everybody look at me!" Don made a run as best an old man could, at the pool. He yelled, "I'm a human cannonball!" as he wrapped both arms about one knee which he had put near his chest as best an old man could. The splash soaked a few onlookers. The cement on one end of the pool darkened as water penetrated the porous concrete. "Help, help me! I've gotten water in my ear an' I can't get out of the pool," According to Don's voice, his predicament warranted immediate medical attention. A boy and a girl dived in to his aid.

"Honey, why I got ya here, I could use a little mouth to mouth. Not you hombre, she gets first dibs."

"I'm not going to kiss you," replied the young lady.

"Fine, smooch on the other guy. See if I care. Just help me get out of the pool before ya pollute the water with your oral love liquid." The young lady pushed on Don's saddle. Denise pulled on the old man's stringy arms. His skin texture resembled a drenched cowboy's worn out lasso. Don had successfully placed two bodies in the pool.

He put a hand on each knee. He breathed. "Ok, mission accomplished." He looked up at Denise. "Time for my nap."

"Not yet. Help me get the water volleyball going and I'll cook you a good pot of stew that a last you all week."

Don took a deep breathe. He was almost ready to speak again.

"Just help me put up the net, Don. You can do it."

Don spoke between exaggerated gasps for air. "I can't move. I going to do cardiac right here, unless." He opened his mouth and wiggled his long tongue, his love thermometer, outside his mouth for the office manager, his nurse, to inspect.

"Fine! I think you're full of hot air. You can blow up the beach ball." Denise and a young gentleman helper began to put up the net.

Don grabbed the ball and began to exhale shallow bursts. His cheeks inflated like balloons. "Hey missy," an attractive female was standing beside him. "Would you blow up my ball? I can't do this sort of thing anymore."

"Sure." She began to inflate the ball.

Don watched. Then out of the blew, he began to talk in perfect Donald Duck fashion. "Oh ya. Oh ya." The young lady tried not to pay attention. "Play with my ball. Play with my ball." The young lady tried not to laugh. Her mouth bounced on and off the input valve to the beach ball. "Don't stop. Don't stop. Oh, that looks so good." He began to quack like a water duck. She puckered down and sucked. She blew. "Show daddy. That's right. Show daddy." He quacked like a duck about to finish shaking the feathers between its legs in something ducks shake their feathers in sometime about spring, when a guy duck does what a duck does to make more ducks. The flock gathered around the simple feat of blowing up a beach ball quacked in laughter.

"You're crazy," replied a dude wearing dry plain short duds.

"Sure, I'm. crazy. It's party time and no time is a party unless ya get a little wild and crazy. Why you can't have a party unless you get crazy, 'cause if you act normal you'd be like all the other times when ya ain't partyin'. Now you're not crazy all the time are you, guy?"

"No."

"Well, there ya go. Now's the time to go crazy. Don't do this at church, though, that would be losin' your marbles crazy. Not a good place to party. Don't ask me how I know." The young man did a cannonball when he jumped in the water.

"Ok, boys and girls follow that guy into the water. You can do it. Pretend like that water has been imported from Los Angeles. Those people from L.A. have no fear of water even if it's cold Pacific shipped from Alaska. I know for a fact this water is plenty warm, and no I didn't take a leak in it," hollered Don as water dripped from his wet shorts down his leg.

Most of the kids jumped in and played with Don's ball that the pretty girl had blown up. Everyone was splashing. Everyone was jumping. Everyone was laughing. The boys watched the girls jiggle their wiggles and the girls gazed back at the boys flexing next to the stretched net. Denise and Don stood next to each other refereeing the carnival of carnal festivities Don the lewd Duck had created.

Denise Johnson turned her eyes away from the pool. In so doing she caught glimpse of a young man walking by himself towards the clubhouse. Given two sidewalks to choose from leading to the clubhouse, he'd chosen to walk on the sidewalk farthest away from the pool area. She watched him drop a check into the rent check deposit box next to the leasing office.

"That's odd."

Don, who had been watching a young lady bouncing up and down in the water, tuned into the office manager on the word 'odd.'

"What's up?"

"That boy. He's been here almost two years. He's never been late on rent before. Usually he's a few days early. Sometimes a week early."

Don pointed at the boy as the youth looked in the opposite direction of the party and began to walk away. "That kid?"

"Ya. His name is John O'Reilly. Keeps to himself. He's kinda of weird."

Something inside Don Murphy's belly moved. The kids around him were laughing, but on the inside he was no longer laughing. The kids around him were playing, but something in him no longer felt like playing. The kids in the pool were having fun, but Don Murphy didn't feel like having any more fun. On the outside Don was a cheerful bouncy boy, but on the inside he was as empty as a completely deflated beach ball. He lifted his cup of beer instinctively like a man who had walked through a desert for days only to discover a pool of saline water from which to drink. With each drink from his cup, the old man's thirst only became greater. He looked at the boy bent over, shoulders slouched and head down. John O'Reilly could have walked better with the assistance of a crutch used by old men, a cane.

Don didn't say anything. He left Denise to have one last summer fling with the residents of Village Green apartments. Don walked as quickly as an old man could towards his apartment, which incidentally, was in the footsteps of the boy in front of him.

He yelled, "Hey kid, wait up!"

The boy heard the man. He did not turn around. He did not take his eyes off the ground. John walked away. Don watched the boy enter apartment building 14452.

Again he yelled, "Hey guy, listen!"

Don watched the entrance door of apartment building 14452 close making building 14452 impervious to his pleas to obtain the attention of the young boy residing within.

CHAPTER 11

Go get the digital video recorder. Here comes the Ward and June Show.

John Jr. O'Reilly, a lad who resembled his father in days long ago just before the dawn of a new century and the twilight of an aged millennium, stared at his parents and little sister at the kitchen table. They were smiling at him. He did not smile back. He was not in the mood to match their gesture. The other three O'Reilly's facial expression was of unequivocal sincerity.

In essence, Mama O'Reilly, Papa O'Reilly, and Kathy's, the girl with golden locks, presence at the table was of complete purity, wholesomeness without any saturated fat or more precisely, steak and eggs for breakfast before one had to worry about clogging a heart with cholesterol. A time when family television meant watching a show where white was white, black was black, good was good, bad was bad, and all the family's concerns, problems, and Beaver's bad grades were discussed over a pleasant seven course meal prepared by June in a white dress and pearls. A time when Ward always sat at the table in his business suit as June had conveniently put supper on the table the second her warrior wearing a tie had walked in the door of their middle class suburban home. Ward, having made income with a briefcase, the only weapon he took to his job, could rely on June to cook some bacon for breakfast the next day with his efforts producing the paycheck before. And she, in turn, was always happy to hand his briefcase to him in the morning when he stepped out the door for yet another day of work.

John, soon to be Ward, was always happy just to see milk in the fridge. So was John Jr.

"Mom, there's no milk! We're out of milk."

Mrs. O'Reilly was caught off guard. She muttered to herself, "There was a gallon of milk in the fridge yesterday." She was shook. She had failed to perform one of her motherly duties. She asked John Jr. the same question she had asked only moments ago but with greater trepidation and much less expectation of receiving a positive response. "We're doing the Ward and June Show. Want to join us?"

The boy started to walk towards the staircase leading to the lower floor of the O'Reilly residence. "Can't Mom. I'm busy. The computer is doing a recompile." He was halfway to the staircase. "Hey Dad, when I got to 12 million on the Nintendo game I found another bug. I think I got it fixed!"

Kathy interrupted the conversation between the Father and his Son. "Daddy, what does recompile mean?"

"Kathy, when a programmer like your brother or Daddy makes a change in a computer program and recompiles we're performing the first step to make the program run without any errors."

"That's great, John! Thanks," the elder O'Reilly yelled in an attempt to extend his voice over the railing of the staircase.

Kathy ran towards her brother. "Can I watch your computer recompile?"

"It's pretty boring, Kat. You can't play the game while I'm recompiling it and it takes almost ten minutes to recompile."

"Kathy, why don't you get your Barbie so we can do the Ward and June Show."

The girl followed her Mother's direction. She ran toward the hallway leading to her bedroom. This hallway, beginning at the staircase, also led to the home's master bedroom adjacent to her room. Both bedrooms were on the same floor of the house as the kitchen.

John Jr. made his way down the staircase. His computer was in his bedroom downstairs. On the last step of the stairway he could hear his winded Mother speak, very gently. He turned around.

"John, what would you like for dinner?"

He yelled back as he rounded the corner of the hallway downstairs, "Pizza's good." and closed the door to his room.

Mrs. O'Reilly could hear the sound of a door closing downstairs. Five steps down the staircase, she turned around, eyeing her husband's feet at the top of the staircase.

"Well, I guess it's the O'Reilly's minus your teenage son, as usual."

"My teenage boy is working on his computer. Let him be."

"I think he plays with that thing too much." Mrs. O'Reilly added for the record as she stomped back up the stairs.

Their daughter joined them. She was ready to play. "I've got my bestest Barbie."

"We've got to get into our outfits. Give us a minute to get changed, Kathy," Mrs. O'Reilly took charge. She would direct the show.

Mr. and Mrs. O'Reilly walked around the corner to the master bedroom and closed the door. John put his suit back on. Mr. O'Reilly watched his wife put on her pearl necklace he had given her on their tenth wedding anniversary. She stood at the mirror atop the dresser examining the fine lines around her eyes. She turned around and looked at her derriere as she pulled on her skirt.

"I think you look simply marvelous for another episode of Ward and June."

She gave no response to his statement. John knew his wife was preoccupied with something beside her figure in the mirror.

"What's bugging you?"

"All your son does is computer stuff. Computer this. Computer that. Dad I just programmed a program that programs itself. Dad I just made a computer that makes other computers." She looked at her husband. "I'm just waiting for him to say, 'My computer is my best." She stopped. "John, your son doesn't have enough friends." She stopped. "He's fifteen. He needs a." She stopped again. "You know. One of those types of friends," as she waived her hand trying to point in the direction of the mirror in front of her.

John O'Reilly took his wife's concerns about the well being of their son lightly. "No problem, me and my boy will find a good web site on the World Wide Web. He'll get his first date in less than fifteen minutes flat. I even think there is a site tailored just for his circumstance, ww.firstdaterealfast.com. Piece of cake."

The hue of her face reddened slightly. She was not pleased with the concern, or lack thereof, her husband displayed over the matter. "And there is something you should know about your son's schoolwork."

John opened his mouth to speak. His little girl interrupted by knocking on the door.

"I'm ready. Daddy, Mommy are you ready, yet?"

Mama and Papa O'Reilly both opened the door and smiled at each other with complete serenity.

"Ward, here is your briefcase. Go outside. Don't forget to ring before you enter."

"Yes, June." John replied with a sarcastic smile.

"You don't get to do any sarcasm, Ward. Now do you character right."

"That's right, Daddy," echoed his daughter.

Mrs. and Miss O'Reilly waved goodbye to Ward Cleaver. Ward dragged his briefcase. He dragged his feet. June watched her weary warrior walk.

"Ward never drags his butt like that."

"That's right, Daddy."

"Do you need a little kick, I mean push, dear?"

"Mommy, can I kick this time?"

Ward wasted no time getting outside. He looked at the yard. He needed to get the leaves raked. Today was garbage day. No one had picked up the trashcan, which now rested in the middle of the yard, next to some bushes. Maybe he could get it tomorrow. Tonight, someone might assume it to be just a large shrub. The neighbor's college kid had parked his 1995 Accord on the curb next to O'Reilly residence. Maybe he should get a Honda. He examined the twenty-year old vintage vehicle. Incredible how a car missing a rear bumper, had a hood painted in primer, and a passenger side mirror held on with tape would start every morning. He assumed the college kid had an early morning class. The jalopy was never there when Ward went to work. He exhaled. Time to stand straight, buckle up, and do the Cleaver. Ward rang the doorbell.

He could hear feet running. Lots of feet. He looked through the door window. Kathy and the O'Reilly's dog, Pluto, were neck and neck in a footrace with the entrance way as a finish line. Kathy broke ahead. With every once of strength a four-year could muster, she yanked the door open. Even if the O'Reilly castle gate had been bolted, she applied enough energy to the door to take it off its hinges.

She jumped up and down. "Daddy's home! Daddy's home! Daddy! Daddy! Daddy!"

Ward smiled back. He kneeled to take a hug. "Hi, Pumpkin! How's my little kitten?"

"Daddy would you look at my picture I painted at school today. Daddy, I drew a snowflake. Daddy, I played hopscotch with Sally and Katy. Daddy, instead of making a series of interconnected boxes we drew a multidimensional snowflake."

"Multidimensional?"

"Yes. Mrs. Jones liked our design. She said Sally, Katy, and I draw very well. We played a new derivation of hopscotch. Daddy, did you know derivation means a change from the existing form?"

"Well, Thanks for telling me. That's wonderful kitten. Sounds like you've had a great day."

June walked up to Ward kneeling next to the opened door. Pluto took advantage of Ward's special time with kitten to slip outside. The dog went directly to the bushes in the center of the yard and preoccupied his nose with the special bush the garbage man had planted earlier today.

"Ward, how was you're day today?" June took her husband's briefcase.

"June, I had a hectic day. Oh, the business meeting I had today. But the sunshine was terrific. It was a wonderful day. How was you're day, dear?"

"Wonderful! I had a wonderful day, as well. I'm so glad you're home, Ward. A few things have come up why you we're gone today." June added a hint of urgency to the last sentence.

"Oh, what sort of things?" Ward deepened his voice by an additional octave to give his belt another notch of manliness needed to tackle any problem whatsoever, no matter how complex. Time to take it like a man. He hated this part of the Ward and June Show.

"Ward, the garbage collector threw the garbage can in the middle of the yard. What are you going to do about it, Ward?"

"Why, I'm going to get the garbage can first thing in the morning and put it in the garage where it belongs."

"Ward, shouldn't you put it away tonight?"

"Ya Daddy, you can't leave the garbage can outside. That's bad, Daddy."

"I'll put that garbage can away tonight." He looked outside through the entrance door's center glass piece slightly fogged from the chill in the air. Maybe he could figure a way to get Pluto to put the trashcan in the garage. The dog liked whatever once was inside the trashcan. He could tell. Only the dog's tale was visible. Fido wagged his tail with the same speed as when his master poured food in the dog bowl.

"Ward, the neighbor's son is parking that, that, awful car next to our yard. What are you going to do about it, Ward?"

"Why, that boy is just trying to get through school, June. I'll talk to him the next time I see him." Ward thought to himself. He hadn't seen the college kid since Labor Day. Chances were really good Ward could avoid any confrontation until next Labor Day. He smiled. June only gave him two "Ward, what are you going to do about its." Easy. Now it was his turn.

"What's for supper, June?"

"I'm not done yet, Ward." She changed her tone. Her voice had been comical with a hint of calamity mixed with distress. The comedy fell short on the next statement. "Ward, you need to take a look at Junior's report card."

Ward didn't want to deal with junior's report card right now. Ward wanted supper. This was the only part of the Ward and June Show he really enjoyed.

"I'm so hungry I'll eat anything you cook me."

"Daddy, you're suppose to say, 'You're so hungry, you could eat a cow. Get it right, Daddy."

"I'm so hungry, I could eat a cow!"

"Don't look at me. I'm tired. I've worked all day, too."

"No Mommy, you're suppose to say, 'Dinner is ready. I just put a pot roast on the table.'"

"Well, I'd put a roast on the table if you're Father would bring home some bacon. Where's the bacon at Ward?"

June had done her job. She had set Ward up like she'd never done before. Now it was Ward's turn. This was the part of the Ward and June Show Kitten enjoyed the most. Ward was going to do his best to make his child chuckle. He stuck out his lower jaw exposing his lower teeth. He strained to pull his eyeballs lower in their socket and in so doing make his brow more pronounced. He slumped over allowing his arms to hang to the point where his hands could touch his knees.

"I'm prehistoric Ward. Get food. Ug." Prehistoric Ward grunted. His daughter giggled.

"Look at Daddy! Mommy, look at Daddy!"

"Ug. Get food. Ug. Feed Family. Where get food? Need get food."

Kathy raised her Barbie and pointed toward the refrigerator.

"Good place get some food." Neanderthal Dad lumbered over to the fridge. He changed slightly with each step. He took each step more cautiously than the next, but with authority, not fear. He scanned to the right and left. He was looking for something, as he inched towards the fridge. His hands no longer dangled. He was holding something, something that allowed him to walk with authority.

"Be very quiet. I'm hunting wabbit."

"Look Mommy! Daddy is Elmer Fudd!"

Elmer Fudd reached in the fridge, without peeking, with the full confidence he had snared a rabbit. He grabbed the first thing that wasn't stuck to the fridge.

"Eureka! I've caught a wabbit!"

"No Daddy, that's a bottle of Heinz ketchup."

Elmer, not wanting to be known as a dud, tossed the plastic squeeze jar to Mrs. Fudd like he knew what he was doing. Mrs. Fudd, in turn, placed the ketchup on the table.

Elmer, pretending to be blindfolded, once again reached inside the fridge. He reached a couple of times. Better try the icebox.

"I've got a wabbit now!" He pulled out a box without looking at the cardboard container and showed it to his little fuddy duddy.

"Daddy caught some fish sticks, Mrs. Pauls. Six of them."

Mrs. O'Reilly's mouth was open in awe. Her daughter had found out how many items were in the box before Mom Fudd even knew what was inside the box. Both lady Fudds clapped their hands. Mr. Fudd bowed in response to the applause.

"I'll nuke the sticks as an appetizer. Six fish sticks for four people isn't enough. Kat, what else do you want for supper?"

"I want Chinese."

The teenager wanted pizza. The child prodigy wanted Chinese food. Maybe June should have put a roast on the table and told them both it was time to eat, take it or leave it. She had tried this course of action. They always left her seven course meal on the table. She watched her husband pour toasted oat grain cereal into a bowl. He was going to eat cereal without milk and without a spoon.

"Ward, one of your kids wants Chinese and the other kid wants pizza. What are you going to do about it, Ward?"

Ward grunted. "Eat Cheerios."

CHAPTER 12

They meet, but she's not interested in his…his evening meal.

What could he do on a Saturday night? He needed to do something. He didn't feel like doing anything. He looked outside through the half open blinds of his patio sliding glass door. From the sun's position, he judged the time to be very late in the afternoon. The lights were not turned on. The room in which sat was slowly becoming darker. He needed to turn on the lights. He didn't feel like getting up to turn on the lights. He'd been looking at page 472 of Upgrading and Repairing PCs for an hour. He didn't feel like reading. He needed to do some reading. He was only a third of the way through the book. What else could he do on a Saturday night?

He thought. He thought of nothing as he stared at a blank wall. He almost smiled though he could not. Thinking of nothing meant he was thinking of something, namely nothing. From this nothingness, something occurred to him. There was a routine he normally did today. He hadn't done it today. He hadn't checked the mailbox. Probably empty. Most of the time the mailbox was empty, but checking the mail was something to do.

He stood up from his chair, slowly, using his arms to lift, as his knees were sore from kneeling at the supermarket all day. He turned the doorknob on his apartment door. He heard another door open, the door to the apartment building, five feet away his the apartment door.

Should he go outside?

Maybe he would wait until whoever opened the door went into their apartment. He didn't feel like meeting anyone, but he needed to meet someone. He'd worked at Schnucks all morning, stocking shelves in the back room. He'd spoken twenty words to someone beside himself today. Half of those words were 'hi' and 'bye'. The others he couldn't remember. He didn't feel like talking to anyone, but thought he needed to talk to someone.

He walked out of his apartment into the hallway. He looked down at the carpet. He didn't need to look up to find his mailbox on the wall adjacent to his apartment. On the carpet next to the row of mailboxes were two bare feet. The feet belonged to a female. The toenails were painted bright red. Footprints were visible on the carpet. He saw water dripping from the owner's legs. The skin of her legs was white and pure in complexion. Her legs were shapely. Pleasing with the brief glance he gave. He looked up. The only garments she was wearing were a pair of cutoff blue jeans and a bikini top. Her hips were full. Her bosom was not. Her hair was sandy brown, straight, reaching nearly to her bosom. She was sifting through a hand full of letters she had received. John stood next to her at the row of mailboxes and opened his mailbox. No mail.

"Hi!" she smiled at John who was two feet away from her, just outside of her zone of intimacy, the space considered to belong to one's body.

"Hi." He tried to smile. He couldn't. He tried to think of something to say. He couldn't.

"I just came back from the pool. What a wild party, that was."

John responded with a mild smirk, a smirk that was his attempt at a smile. She, in turn, refrained from smiling further.

"What's your name?"

"John."

She waited a few seconds for him to say something. She waited for him to say his last name. She waited for him to ask her what her name was. The silence became uncomfortable.

"So what do you do, John?"

"Do?"

"You know. Where do you work at?"

"Oh." John pepped up a bit. His slouched shoulders straightened. Maybe she wanted to talk. Maybe she was interested in him. Maybe she wanted to get to know him.

"I'm a computer technician at Best Buy and I'm a stocker at Schnucks."

"Oh." She looked down the hallway away from John like someone had caught her attention. "Well, speaking of Schnucks, I need to make something to eat before I go out tonight. Have to run." She sprung down the hallway. Halfway to the apartment adjacent to his she turned around, smiled, and said, "Nice meeting you."

No sooner had John turned the lock on his mailbox and turned around to open his mouth to say 'goodbye' was the female, whose name he did not know, in her apartment, the apartment next to his. John ate some cereal, generic no name brand toasted oats, that night for supper. He didn't feel like watching TV. He didn't feel like reading. He went to bed early that Saturday, two days before Labor Day. Tomorrow was Sunday, his fishing day. He didn't feel like fishing, even if the day was perfect for fishing. He didn't feel like doing anything on the one day he could do as he pleased.

CHAPTER 13

Doris thinks he's Dad. Don thinks he's her sugar Dad.

Time to write. He was past due. Don Murphy wanted to get started by five tonight. A little indigestion pushed him behind schedule an hour. He needed an after dinner drink to get rolling, something beside the twenty plastic cups filled to the rim with beer now chilling in the fridge. He'd pilfered two at a time why Denise wasn't looking. The ten trips he had made between the keg and his apartment, had made those greasy party burgers roll around in his stomach, releasing some acid.

Never again, he told himself, would he eat one of Denise's burgers. Maybe one, but he wasn't going to eat ten in a row like he did this afternoon. On the plus side, he looked so hungry she promised to make him not only a fresh pot of stew for each day of this week but for the next week as well. He had a few tricks up his sleeves, lines she'd never heard before, to convince her to extend her hospitality. Dinner was taken care of until the end of September. By then he'd have a new game plan for a free meal deal cooked up. He grabbed a bottle of Tums, not opened until this afternoon, but which was now, at seven o'clock, almost empty.

His hands trembled as he touched the keys on his typewriter. He was thirsty for some scotch. His belly ached. He cursed his age and predicament. Had he been twenty years younger he would have carried the whole keg to his apartment, doing away with all that horrible walking making his tummy feel like the inside of a grill filled with red hot charcoal coals. He needed a little firewater, a good shot of whiskey, to put out the flames inside his stomach.

"I got it! Love of fire. A mountain man, falls in love with a native Indian chief's daughter. He wants to ride off into the sunset with her. She's cool with it because he's got a tomahawk

86

painted like she's never seen before. But first, the chief makes the guy walk on hot coals of fire, to test his manhood, make sure he's good enough for his girl, doesn't cry like a sissy, all that bullshit."

He began to write, "Chapter 1." He hit the carriage return on his typewriter. "Ok, first sentence. The air was still as." He stopped hitting the keys. "As still as. As still as a quiet morning on a lone mountain in the forest he'd never seen the likes of before. Not even the crickets chirped. He. Nope, I need a name. Something to do with Indians. Got it. John whatever."

The keys of the typewriter stopped making noise. "How 'bout, John Bushmaster. Nope. How 'bout John Firemaker. Too prehistoric. How 'bout Solewalker. That's it! John Solewalker." Don Murphy hit at the keys once again, pausing to search for the 'w' key.

"He walked cautiously through the foliage, taking great care not to disturb the litter of leaves beneath him." He stopped typing, noting he had misspelled a word.

"That sucks. Solewalker sucks. Need a cool name like,like dammit! I'm offkey!" He ripped the page from the typewriter.

He stared at the ceiling, and lifted his arms as he spoke to the blank wall above him. "Give me a name, dammit! Just give me a name. That's all I need."

His apartment became as quiet as one can be when a man alone in his den stops speaking to himself. He spoke again to fill his room with sound. "Give me a sign. Anything. That's all I need. Is that asking a lot from you?" He shook his fist at the ceiling and cursed.

Don Murphy got his sign that Saturday evening in the form of a ring, followed by another ring, and yet another. The phone was ringing. Someone was calling Don Murphy.

Don looked at the telephone number displayed on the caller id. The number didn't belong to any first rate New York publisher or even a bottom of the barrel paperback producer. The girl in the apartment building next door was calling. This was the third time in four days. Why had he talked to her in the first place? She wasn't a publisher. He grinned. He knew why he'd whipped up a little conversation espresso with her on her way to her car two weeks ago. She was young. She was cute. Those two items were a winning combination and always aroused a brew of emotion he enjoyed like a coffee connoisseur savors a cup of good coffee, very steamy and very hot. He picked up the phone.

"Hi Doris."

"How'd ya know it was me?"

"Oh, just a lucky hunch. I can always tell when a young lady as lovely as a tulip in full bloom is tiptoeing at my telephone."

"Oh, Mr. Murphy. The things you say. You're so. So poetic."

"I'm a seasoned man. Being well versed is just one of many skills, with time, I have mastered."

"You're such a wise man, Don. I'm so glad I can talk to you. You give such good advice."

Don thought to himself. "Dammit! Wise men have gray hair. Wise men are old. Wise men don't jump into the sack with the tulip tootsie. Wise men need a cane to get out of bed, the only stiff thing they hold onto in the morning. Might as well get this over with."

He spoke aloud, "What's troubling your young heart this evening? How has a man upset the pulse of the life you so yearn to be filled with love?"

"Don, how do you know these things?"

Don thought. "Because that's all you ever call to talk about. How your boyfriend is making your life the pits. How your boyfriend doesn't want to go horseback riding and you want to so you call me up because I know how to get your boyfriend to take you horseback riding. How your boyfriend doesn't pay you enough attention so you call me up because I know how to get your boyfriend to pay more than enough attention to you. How your boyfriend and you don't talk enough on the telephone but I talk to you on the telephone for hours. I'm doing all the work here, and getting none of the rewards. I should be your boyfriend. Might as well go ahead and play the old guy with wisdom card."

Don spoke. "Your voice trembles with the tumult of love's waves when broken upon the rocks of a desolate seashore of despair."

She vented, releasing hot air from her mouth. "Tony hasn't called yet this evening. I told him to call me by six. That was over an hour ago. I don't know. I'm not sure he's."

Mr. Murphy interrupted. She didn't even give him a complement on his best Shakespeare shit. She ignored it. "Don't know what?" Don answered his own question. "Don't know what time it will," he paused to breathe.

She interrupted, "No, Don. I know what time it is. It's 7:18pm. I don't know why he hasn't called." Her voice hesitated. "I don't know about Tony."

Don thought about completing his sentence, "be when you'll get a phone call from him?" He didn't bother. It was time to dish out some standard issue fatherly advice. "I think Tony, the pizza boy, is a fine young man."

"He's the manager of a Dominoes Pizza, he's not just a pizza boy. What do you really thing of him, Don?"

"I've never met him."

"Well, from what I've told you about him."

Don thought. "On the even days of the month he's the greatest man ever to make dough West of the Mississippi. On odd days of the month this guy's gonna be flatter than a pancake if he has to go out with you, the wicked witch of the East. If I was this guy, Tony the tiger, I'd be hangin' with his cool cat friends, and figurin' out a way to catch a new kitty cat. Which is why he hasn't called."

Don spoke. "Doris, give him some time to call. It's only seven. The eve has only begun. Don't be so inflexible. Give your Romeo a few more drops of sands from the hour glass to come hither to your balcony."

"Mr. Murphy, you're right. You give such sound advice."

"I know."

"You know what it is? I think I'm more serious about the relationship than Tony. Tony's fun to be around, but I'm more serious than he is. Do you think so, too?"

Don finally spoke what he thought. "What are you so serious about? You've known this guy for what? Two months. You need to lighten a little. In fact, You know what it is? What you need is a casual name, something more carefree, more fun than Doris, something which will make you sore to new heights of lightness."

He thought. "How 'bout something which rhymes with balloons. This girl got more hot air to fill a balloon than even me."

He spoke. "What's your middle name, Miss Dugan?"

"Denise." She handed over the middle name feebly, still recovering from being told she lacked lackadaisicalness.

"Easy as pie. I pronounce you Deedee, the first letter of your first name followed by the first letter of your second name. From here on call yourself Deedee and the boys will beckon to your calling machine promptly."

"You think so?"

"Deedee, I know so."

He thought for a second about dishing out some more poetry. Why bother? She wasn't eating. Don decided to appear to take concern in Deedee Dugan's well being. Might as well play the 'concern' card.

"Are you going to continue to deliver pizza, now that the summer's end is nearing?"

"I guess so. It works into my schedule. My classes are during the day. My clinicals at school next semester are all day, too. The money is all right. I made a hundred last night, and since I'm seeing Tony."

"The pizza guy?"

"He's the manager, Mr. Murphy."

"So you're pretty much set until next summer."

"Yes, and next summer I'll be working at the clinic full time."

"I see. How does Tony fit into the picture come next spring?"

"I don't." Her speech slowed. "know." It picked up again. "Do you think Tony and I make" She stopped. She hesitated to say what she wanted to say. She wanted to talk about her boy friends, but not necessarily Tony. She whined like a little girl who can't get what she wants. "I just can't seem to meet any men who are right for me."

Don thought. "I knew it. Now where getting somewhere. I should have played the 'I care' card from the start. Time to sound like Mr. Knowledgeable. Let's test the water."

He spoke. "What you need is a man with more flare, more gusto, more pizazz than the pizza guy. These Midwest boys are too dry. There's not enough water around here. What you need is an East Coast man."

"Really. Maybe you're right, Don."

"Of course, I'm right. People from out East are more you're flavor. You see everyone has a shell, an outer superficial personality they expose to everyone. Only after breaking this shell will a person speak what they think. You have to get through this barrier before someone will reveal their true conscience, their innermost thoughts and desires. Understand?"

"Yes." She didn't give much thought to saying the word. "What's that have to do with men from the East Coast?"

"People from the Midwest are conservative. That shell covers nearly their entire personality. When you talk to someone from the Midwest for the first time all you get is 'hi', the time, the weather, and 'bye.' That's what makes them so dry. The shell is easy to break because it's got a lot of personality to cover, but you've got to know how. East Coast people, on the other hand, expose many more layers of their personality, putting that shell, a tougher one, way down deep around the core of their being. So, you see, an East Coast man is more friendly, more fun to be around since they've got a better exposed personality."

Don thought. "Time to put my toe in the pool. How hot is that water?"

91

"By the way, I've spent a long time in New York City. I'm practically from the East Coast."

"I don't know about that Mr. Murphy. I spent a week in Washington D.C. three years ago with my sister. From what I saw of riding the subway, people aren't as friendly there as they are here."

Mr. Murphy muttered a curse word to himself as he thought. "Sure they are, you've just gotta point a gun at 'em, that's all! Then they'll start talking. As a matter of fact, they won't stop talking, screaming, or instinctively reaching into their back pockets and purses."

Deedee wanted to say something before Don started his shell game. She was still hesitant. "Joe Barnes says he went to an Ivy League school. He's going to medical school at Washington University." She paused. "I really liked your joke about the three beers." She spoke softly. Don was barely able to hear her, "Did he say anything about me?"

Don thought. "What? Goldilocks, you didn't like my joke this afternoon. Joe Cool eyeing you? You need to get your feet back on the ground. I've had it. This is a waste of time." A light bulb lit up in his mind.

Don spoke. "How about that guy." He hunted for a word. "John. He lives in your apartment building on your side."

"Who?"

"John, I met him at Schnucks a few days ago."

"Oh. The computer nerd next door to me?" She laughed incredulously. "He's a dwebe," she hissed back at Donald Murphy.

Don thought. "Dwebe. Dwebe. Oh yeah. I coined that word when I was working on. What book was that? Hives in the Summer Fields? What year? What year? 1978?"

Don spoke. "Deedee, you'll have to help this old man. I don't understand everything you kids say nowadays."

"Ya know. A loser. Don, hold on just a second, I just got another phone call." A minute later she spoke quickly. "It's Tony. He called. You were right. I've gotta go. Talk to ya later!"

What Doris Denise Dugan didn't know was she had hung up the telephone on a man who had a collection of a thousand books of the type found in the paperback section of a supermarket, the kind of book with a shirtless handsome man on the front cover clutching a voluptuous love bitten woman in his arms. Nor did she know why Don Murphy had become such a collector of supermarket romance novels.

Don Murphy had a thought. Something of a sneaky one. Could be considered something sly, maybe even almost sinister. He found the name in the phone book easy enough. John O'Reilly said just one word to his question. "Ya."

With this word, Don Murphy unknowingly took his first step to walking further than one can walk in sixty years or even six hundred years. Don was taking his first step to putting some humane in his being, something to fill the inside of his shell, which was, at this point in his life, filled only with void. He was about to get more of life than one can in a lifetime. He stopped writing that night. For the first time in a long time his mind was filled with too many thoughts to put on paper. He was going to do some fishing with one of his neighbors tomorrow.

CHAPTER 14

There's a fortune in pizza.

"Honey, supper is almost ready." Mrs. O'Reilly looked at her husband's back as he pecked at the keyboard of his computer.

"Ok, I'll be there in just a minute."

"Ward, I knocked on the door to your son's room almost ten minutes ago. He said the same thing you just did. But he's not in trouble like you!"

Ward dug his head out of his computer screen and twisted his neck like an ostrich looking at a hungry hyena. "What'd I do, now?"

"This is the second time I've told you supper's ready! You can play with you're computer after you eat. Go tell your son its suppertime. I'll have the fishsticks fried by the time you two sit down at the table."

June watched a disgruntled Ward stand up and walk out of the den. "Your son was talking on the telephone when I checked." She turned to Kathy who had one hand on the microwave remote control. "Not yet Kathy. Wait for Daddy to go downstairs." Kathy sat at the kitchen table flipping through the yellow pages with her other hand.

Ward stood at the staircase. "Hey John! Supper's ready. Let's eat!"

A voice emanated from downstairs up the staircase. "Just a minute, Dad."

June gave her husband a frown as he walked down the staircase. "Good luck. Remember we can't microwave the sticks twice because the imitation cheese stuff inside will turn into rubber. You must get you're son out of his bedroom fortress within thirty seconds with a ten second cool down period taken into account." She turned to Kathy. "Ok, start the microwave!"

Ward knocked on his son's door. "Supper's being nuked as I speak. Want to eat?"

"Dad, I'm busy. I'm programming."

"You can program the computer after you eat."

"But Dad." John O'Reilly's son opened the door to his room. He had a visor, the latest in computer imaging equipment, over his eyes.

"Take the visor off and put your portable laptop under your shirt so your Mom doesn't see. I won't tell her your programming but you'll have to come up with your own excuse to why you're looking at your lap while we eat dinner."

The four O'Reilly's sat at the kitchen table eating their fishstick and ketchup. John Jr. spoke first. "Where's the pizza?"

Kathy whizzed from the section of the phone book containing the c's for Chinese to the section containing the p's for pizza. Her finger ran through the phonebook, sifting pertinent information from the meaningless. The other three O'Reilly's opened their mouth, but before Mama or Papa or Junior could speak Kathy put a taste on the tip of their tongue. "How about Chinese Pizza?"

"How did you do that?" the elder John spoke with a dry mouth produced from the thought of having to eat two types of food that when combined had produced the most horrendous experiment in the O'Reilly refrigerator to date.

"There is no such thing as Chinese Pizza," replied the younger John.

"Those two ingredients being mixed sounds a lot like cooking. You know Mommy doesn't like cooking."

"I did a alphabetical search like Mommy showed me how to." Kathy pointed at the listing in the phone book for her brother to see. "Mommy, it says straight from the wok to your door in ten minutes or it's flee."

"Flea? You mean free don't you, Kathy?" Kathy showed her mother the ad in the yellow pages. "Must be a typo. Well, if it's already cooked it's good for me, how about you boys?"

Mr. O'Reilly replied, "I guess we can try something new."

John Jr. took a big gulp, "What kind of toppings do you get?"

Kathy was already on the phone. "Is this the Wok Express?" She spoke again. "We want pizza. What comes on top?" She looked at her brother. "Is flied lice OK?"

"See if we can get sweet and sour sauce, too."

Kathy spoke into the phone and replied to her brother, "Mr. Chow says he uses only the finest sweet and sour tomato paste so the lice will stay on the doe."

"OK."

The O'Reilly's waited five minutes for their pizza. Kathy read the lid on the newly delivered pizza box. "Wok Express doesn't deliver just another cheesy pizza." Three O'Reilly's began to cautiously eat.

The teenage O'Reilly engulfed. Between swallows he spoke, "Mind if I get another piece?"

Mrs. O'Reilly hurried to get in some conversation with her son. "So how was school today?" Her son did not look up. He was staring at his lap.

He swallowed. "OK."

"Did you do anything in school today?"

He gulped. "Not much."

"Who were you talking to on the phone before dinner?"

He exhaled. "I was chatting on the Internet."

"Is that a computer in you're lap?"

"No, Mom. I'm reading the phone book."

"No, you're not. Your sister has the phone book in her lap. You can chat on your computer when you're done with dinner."

John Jr. swallowed one last time. "I'm done with dinner."

"Wait a second. Stick around for the fortune cookie, Son."

Kathy reached over the table and grabbed the fortune cookie originally placed in the center of the pizza. She read, "The family that eats together, burps together."

Mrs. O'Reilly replied, "Kathy, it's the family that eats together stays together."

John Jr. read the fortune. "She's right, Mom."

"They'll be no burping at this table."

Mr. O'Reilly looked at his boy. "Son, how 'bout you and I go downstairs, belch a few, sav'em as sound files, and broadcast them over the Internet."

CHAPTER 15

The boy is on the edge of a new day.

He opened his eyes. Before him was a ledge. The same edge he had seen time and time before when he awoke waited for him patiently to move this Sunday the day before Labor Day. He did not look over it, but he could not overlook this ledge before his eyes, the border of which was within a blade's length of his whisker filled neck. He was motionless, and in turn, this ledge, his nemesis, did the same, like a tiger crouched in thick grass.

He could tell what was on the horizon, what kind of day the day would become, vibrant, full of radiance or complete lack thereof, namely dreary precipitation, from the precipice in his face. The light illuminating from around the perimeter of the ledge had existed since the moment of the new day's dawn, neither decreasing or increasing in intensity. He did not know how long ago the day had begun, but he could tell today would be gloomy, having a sky with no sun, yet no moon. Shadows did not exist in this land, a land covered by the curtain of a completely cloud filled day. The glow at the end of the shades next to the Formica windowsill was dull, a slight haze of dim soft light cast over this ledge he looked upon.

He blinked his eyes. He blinked again, and each time his eyes closed longer he dreamt of slumber shorter. He did not sleep. The only motion his body produced with which he was aware was the constant flicker of his eyelids. If he could move, just lift his torso upright. No. Maybe just turn his head to check the time on the alarm clock. No. He could not move. He could open his see eyes to see himself standing on the edge of a steep ledge with but one direction to go, downward, or close his eyes to confront a tiger ready to leap. He could not move. He could not fall asleep.

Something inside him, some small synaptic flicker of thought, gave relief to his anxiety. Someone had called him yesterday evening after he had gone to bed. Another synapse in his brain fired. "Hey kid, you going fishing tomorrow?" It was the old man. John O'Reilly couldn't recall what he said to the man but the old man had responded, "Count me in. I'll go fishing with you, kid." More synapses responded. He had a reason to get out of bed. Someone was waiting for him to go fishing. He could move. He rolled over. 8am. He got out of bed, even though he had no desire to get out bed.

Today he won, but he was exhausted. The tiger had leapt over the cliff when he rolled away from the ledge. Tomorrow would be another struggle. He opened the blinds to look at the clouds blanketing the sky. His forecast of making it out of bed tomorrow was bleaker. He had no anticipation of what tomorrow would bring. He grew weaker, more tired each day, unable to recuperate from the previous day's labors. Something as simple as getting out of bed became a triumph of the will. His will, nearly depleted, was all but defeated. He swallowed his Prozac. He needed more.

He walked to the old man's apartment. He was pessimistic the old man would be there. He was going to knock once, drive his pickup truck to Creve Couer Lake Park, and try to fish all day, or at least sleep in the only place he found solace to soundly sleep, underneath the embracing branches of a lone oak tree. If he could journey to this tree, he could endure another week, weaker though he may be from his last week.

The thirty yards between his apartment building and the old man's dwelling was a trek of a thousand miles through arctic tundra. The ground was damp. Today's dawn had failed to remove the night's condensation from the grass. His old sneakers absorbed the moisture, making his feet become, in his mind, wet concrete blocks slowly hardening. He slugged forward, each step becoming slower than the last.

The old man's patio blinds were open. Light, much brighter than the effervescent glow the new day could produce, pierced through the boundaries of the patio sliding glass door. John didn't remember what time he told the old man he was going fishing. Was the old man awake waiting for him? He looked inside. The blinds were drawn so what appeared to be glowing from a multitude of lights was, in fact, emitting from a single source, a high wattage desktop lamp situated on a table in the kitchen directly in his view.

He squinted. The desk lamp was on no ordinary table. The tabletop was painted with a design he could not discern. Though in the shadows, the four table legs were obviously the silhouettes of the human figure, the precise anatomical details he could not place. On the table were an assortment of papers scattered around a vintage typewriter. The typewriter did not have an electric cord. Next to the typewriter was John O'Reilly's answer. The old man was home. He was not awake.

One arm was draped around the typewriter. At the end of the other arm was an empty bottle the old man had positioned somehow to use as a pillow. The bottle not only propped his face upright, but also, as his cheekbone clung to the curve in the bottle's neck, locked his facial expression in a lopsided lighthearted smile. He looked happy. Permanently. The old man had something on top his head, a hat of unordinary proportions. More than one second elapsed before John could comprehend what his eyes saw. The old man's adornment was a cap with a feather in it. Many feathers. Yankee Doodle Dandy was wearing an Indian chief's headdress. The shadows of the feathers danced on the wall beside him, like little Indians, misguided by the big chief's precarious position on the bottle. These little Indians were ready to make some mischief, to start some fires and put out the flames both at the same time.

John looked at the bottle of firewater the old man clung to for support. He was going to knock once and leave. If the same events as the last time he knocked on this door transpired he would not walk to his truck. He would go back to his apartment, back to his den, a den with a lion waiting for him. As before, the same desire, the same basic need, the need for a friend induced him to tap his hand on the door of the old man's dwelling. He knocked. He waited. He didn't want to look inside the patio as he moped to his vehicle. Time to go. Time to drive to the lake. Keys in the ignition. He couldn't put his truck in reverse. He couldn't go alone. He needed to look inside that bright patio window, glowing with a chance of companionship. He turned around. This time he pounded on the door. The door opened.

"Fishing." The old man looked at him. He looked at the old man. "Want to?"

"Ok, kid. Give me just a minute, that's an hour to you young folk." The old man was completely awake, not partially. John could tell from the energy in the man's voice. He stepped inside the apartment.

"Whoa, whoa, whoa! Hey Tonto, whatdathinkya doin' puttin' those mushy mocassins on my carpet." John looked at his soaked grass laden shoes. "Take 'em off. See those slippers. Put those on."

John looked at the slippers, the same ones he had seen before. The ones with the bunnies bouncing on the end. John didn't move.

"Hey kid, you ever been to Japan?"

"No."

"Well, I have. In Japan land they never walk in the house barefoot. They got stinky feet over there from treading through muddy rice fields barefoot all day. I can tell from just one step you got stinky feet and I ain't even seen 'em."

"I'll wait here."

"Suit yourself, guy. I want you to know what an unbelievable opportunity you have let slip under your feet."

"What?"

"Those slippers were worn by the original creator of Bugs Bunny himself." John looked with disbelief.

"I won 'em in a strip poker game back in '74."

"You were playing strip poker with the creator of Bugs Bunny?"

"Don't give some weird look like I'm a carrot eater, kid. Me and Bugs, that's what they called him, were playing with ten bunnies at the Playboy mansion. I was down to my lucky belt and he was down to his''

"You've been to the Playboy mansion?"

"Hell, kid, lived there for a year. Try 'em on."

John was apprehensive. Was the old man trying to get him to take off more than his shoes?

"Don't look at me like I'm Wacko Jacko. I said, 'Playboy mansion,' not 'Michael Jackson's mansion with the ferry wheel in the backyard.' Look, if I had the hot for little boys, I would have plucked the fruit out of your looms when ya first stepped in the door."

John stared at the bunnies. Not on the slippers next to him, but on the magazine covers atop the coffee table to his right. A year's worth of Hugh Hefner's two dimensional recreation of the female form were spread out on the coffee table. He glanced at the old man. He stared at the magazines.

"Ya know. A Hershey highway hitchhikin' fudge packin' cheek chosin' tallywacker tastin' lollypop lick'n prefers suckin' fudgescicles over squeezin' melons homosexual." John was motionless. "Guy, how many gays do you know who spread out Playboy magazine on their coffee table?"

"None."

"Well, there ya go. That's because homosexuals don't look at Playboy magazine." The old man grinned at John. "Just like playboys don't read Computer Shopper." John didn't say anything. "Try 'em on. Feel soft don't they?"

John nodded. He tried to think of something to say. Only disbelief came to mind. "How did you get so many women to play strip poker with you?"

"Well, it's like this. Me and Bugs were talking in the hall when some real red hot queens wearing lots of diamonds walked by. I said to Bugs as I smiled at their diamonds, 'One with the best pair wins.'"

"They said, 'what do we win?'"

"Bugs says, 'these slippers I got on.'"

"They said, 'you guys are bunch of jokers."

"I says to Bugs, 'brother, I don't know how we are going to pick a centerfold to be in our next movie, Cinderella Catches Doc."

"One of em' replies,' Who are you guys? Because I'm callin' security.'"

"So the security guard shows. What they don't know is we have given the guard two tens and three fives, to say, 'Mr. Hefner's made time in his full schedule for you. He's glad you've come to his house, Mr. Warners.' The brunettes jumped first. I got three on top of me. Bugs got a pair of redheads. They treated us like kings. They stripped us naked faster than a blonde can spell eye."

"What about the blondes?"

"By the time they figured out who we said we were, the only thing left was the club."

"The club?"

"Ya. The guard had a club. They went after him to get the club, and did they do it royally, to flush the brunettes and redheads off us two jokers."

"I still don't understand how you got the slippers."

"I got three of a kind, which beat Bug's pair. Don't you know how to play poker?" the Sheik of Strip Stories then waved his hand and said in perfect Porky Pig fashion, "That's, that's, that's all folks!"

John didn't believe his ears. An incredulous story spoken by a man with an impression of a whiskey bottle molded on his cheek. He watched the old man disappear down the hallway. To his right, adjacent to the coffee table, was a black leather couch. He sat down. The leather was plush and soft, but wrinkled and as ancient as the old man. The contour of the couch was uncomfortable. His shoulders barely rested against the back of the couch. This couch was built not to be sat in, but to lie down upon.

In front of his view, against the far wall, was a television of enormous proportions, a big screen. On top of the screen, to the right of the screen, to the left of the screen, and covering every inch of space on the far wall not occupied by the television were stacks of videocassettes piled three, maybe four layers deep, hundreds, if not a thousand VCR tapes. The television was brand new. The instructions for how to use the remote were on the floor beneath his feet. They had not been removed from the packaging.

He looked to his left. The table with the unusually shaped legs occupied most of the dining area. The details of the leg's contours came into focus. Each leg was molded in the form of a female, standing naked, with one hand holding the table and another holding. He stared. He followed the form's arm to the hand clasping the inner join of the legs. Odd, a hand would be carved with only the ends of four fingers in view. A thought came to mind. He turned his eye's elsewhere. The young man shook his feet. He had taken his first step into a new world wearing the kind of suit a rabbit wore.

The old man reappeared holding a bottle. "What is it kid? You don't believe me do ya? As a matter of fact, you looked like ya just stepped into the wacky ward at the hospital. Ya know. Where they keep all the local looneys."

John didn't say anything.

"See that nudie magazine in the middle? Ya that one, Miss March '74. What turns her on?

"Turns her on?"

"Ya know. Wets her whistle, shakes her caboose loose. Makes her dance till dawn, makes her so horny she'll kiss the warts off a toad." John provided no feedback. The old man sighed, "What arouses her. That's her handwriting on the page opposite her naked butt."

John read aloud the centerfold's 'turn ons turn offs' section. "Gentleman wearing slippers. A man named Donny is simply irresistible." John looked up.

The old man had walked behind the table with the legs and the torso, too, but missing part of a finger. He pointed one finger straight up in the air. Caesar was about to speak before a crowd of citizens in the forum. With the other hand he waived his bottle at a bookcase behind the table. In particular, he pointed at the top row of the bookcase, a row with at least a hundred books. John counted the number of rows, ten, all filled with books, in the expansive book container, both in height and width. The old man, donning a vest, put the bottle on the table and grabbed the edge of his vest like great orators do when about to expound the opening remark of a speech destined to be written by the hands of history.

"I am." He paused to examine the expression of the boy's face. "Donald," he looked again and pointed his Caesar finger higher in the air. "Darren!" Maestro Murphy waived his finger as a conductor does to keep his orchestra in harmony. John showed no inclination to follow the old man's exuberant tempo. The old man thrust his finger directly overhead for the finale anyway, "Murphy!"

The finale flopped. John didn't vibrate. He didn't move. He heard no symphony.

"Ya never heard of me? The great one and only Murphy? Awe, the hell with it! You, damn kids don't read nothin' nowadays. All you do is tune into music television and eat junk food all day long! Back in my day if you wanted to turn the channel you had to flip open a new book. Ya know. Turn a page. And if ya wanted some potato chips you had to dig 'em up yourself, chop a tree for wood, walk six miles to town through the snow to get a pot to boil 'em in, make your own knife by smelting some iron from the pot, peel the potato with the knife ya made, save the peelings and glue 'em together to make shoes for the winter so you could walk back to town in the snow to return the pot with the hole in it which ya got to keep 'cause the neighbor didn't want a hole in his pot so ya had to give away all the potato chips ya made to make the neighbor happy except for one small wafer thin slice of a potato. But ya know what? By that time ya were too damn tired to open ya mouth to swallow."

Don walked back into the kitchen with the bottle mumbling something about eating tree chips when he was a child, wearing socks made out of potato skins, underwear made out of tree bark, and hating warm weather because the bugs would bite in his britches, and the cold weather being even worse since everyone would call him Mr. Potato head because his hat was made from potatoes, too.

"Where is a maid when you need one. I want a wife. Hey kid, you mind givin' me a hand in the kitchen?" A minute elapsed before Don Murphy reappeared from the kitchen. "Kid, what da ya say? I could use your help filling up my bottle. I don't see like I used to."

John walked into the kitchen. Nothing out of the ordinary except a mangled fork. The countertops were clean. There was nothing on the countertops. No snacks, no dirty dishes, no spices, nothing except a coffee maker in the corner next to the sink. The old man had the refrigerator door open. John looked inside. The contents of the frig matched what was on the countertops, that is, there was nothing in the frig. No mustard or mayonnaise, milk or iced tea, or even a leftover. Only one item. Beer. Just beer. About twenty cups worth all lined neatly on the bottom shelf, the only shelf.

"My doctor told me to give him a urine sample when I see him next week. Man, does that guy get pissed at me when I say, 'What's up Doc?'" Don nibbled on the phrase in perfect Bugs Bunny fashion. "He says I have a drinking problem. Damn right, I got a drinking problem. All of these cups are full of alcohol, but one of 'em I wouldn't want to drink from. Now that's a problem."

John opened his eyes wide. He was about to shake his head to and fro.

"I'm not askin' ya to sample my beer, kid. Can ya tell a difference by lookin'?"

John looked. He tried. "No."

"Dukie. Diarrhea. Kid, I need a bottle of." He examined John's facial expression. "Pepto-Bismol. I'm short on change. Got any? We're going fishin', right?"

"Ya."

Don walked into his bedroom. "Should put on my fishing hat. Never can tell when the Sun will come out in St. Louis. Where we going fishing anyway?" He returned wearing a toupee.

"Creve Couer Lake in Maryland Heights."

"So we've got to get off of I-270 at the Dorsett exit?"

"Ya."

"Holmes, the game is afoot!"

The old man hurried towards the door. John O'Reilly followed, barely keeping step with the over exuberant hound in search of something pink to drink. John, with bloodshot eyes, reached to close the sleuth's apartment door. The old man grabbed hold of the boy's arm as if he had nabbed his rival nemesis, Dr. Moriarty.

"Hey kid, don't forget to put your sneakers back on. People will look funny at ya if ya walk 'round outside wearin' Bug's slippers." He smiled at the young man. "Don't ask me how I know."

CHAPTER 16

John don't know it, Don's a poet.

There was almost no movement in the city of St. Louis. Rarely did a vehicle go by John O'Reilly's truck as he drove to Creve Couer Lake. Not a single person could be seen outside their residence. Some interior house lights were lit. Whether these lights had inadvertently been left on from the previous night or where turned on to assist lighting the morning could not be discerned. There was no indication any inhabitants where stirring in their homes. The day had come, but everyone was asleep. John had felt the same stillness several Sundays before with but one difference. He had a passenger with him this time, and Don Murphy was anything but quiet.

Don had turned on the radio. He was channel surfing, seeking the station, the song, which matched his driver's mood. He didn't ask to turn on the radio. He didn't ask if he had the volume too loud, until John had to read Don's lips to understand. Don lowered the sound level.

"Man, did I sleep good last night. I haven't had such a solid night's rest since the night after I got out of jail in '71."

John's hands tightened around the steering wheel.

"Relax, kid. It's not liked I killed someone, only spent a weekend in the slammer for falling asleep at the wheel, which looks like what you were about to do. Can you believe that, haven't slept that well in nearly. How old you anyway, kid."

"Twenty three."

"I haven't slept so well befo' you born."

John nodded his head, but this time to confirm he was awake.

Don looked at his chauffeur. The boy looked like he was driving a hearse. He was driving. Somewhere. Someplace he had gone to time and time again. He could do it in his sleep. He looked ahead, but his eyes weren't on the road. Don went back to channel surfing on the radio.

"Kid, you look like you've been listening nonstop to the station with the blues playing twenty four hours a day."

"St. Louis doesn't have a blues station."

"Can you believe that. I think you're right. Let's see if I can find the next best thing." Don found a country music radio station. He listened for just a second, and started singing the tune in unison to the song writer, but with slightly different words, "I've still got with me my dog named Rover, 'cause my wife done left an' moved to Dover. We're eating out of the same can of spam, because fido cannot cook worth a damn. Now that dog got a really long tongue with which he do like to lick, but I'll never get so desperate to do that to my own."

John rolled down the window to let some fresh air in. His eyes returned to the road ahead. A drop of clear liquid was stuck on the edge of the windshield. Maybe some condensation? Then another drop appeared. And another, ever so miniscule. Maybe something had been poured on the highway. He looked at the asphalt pavement of the interstate. Dry. The slightest of mist, inch by inch, covered the entire windshield. The drops did not interfere with his visibility of the road. He didn't want it to rain. He didn't want to go back to his apartment. He didn't want to turn on his wipers and admit the day was too wet to go fishing.

The old man turned to John, "Hey kid, looks like it's gonna rain," He saw some condensation along the rim John O'Reilly's eyes. "Tell ya what, we're at the Dorsett exit. Let's stop at the store up here and see what happens."

John nodded. Don Murphy pointed at a convenience store. John had driven by this store every fishing trip. This was his first time to park in front of Dirt Cheap Beer and Cigarettes.

The old man sank chirped like a canary about to fly the coop, "Cheap, Cheap. Fun. Fun. Dirt Cheap Beer and Cigarettes." His voice deepened. "Home of the persecuted smoker and my good 'ol pal Jim Bean. They got the pep." Don's eyes focused on the parking lot. "I need." Like a bird on a wire his neck swung around like he'd been bolted with a million volts. The other half of the parking lot was empty, too. He stopped singin' faster than a canary does just before there's a gas explosion in a coal mine. His eyes bulged to read the store hours sign on the entrance.

"Oh, shit! Kid, what day is it?"

"Sunday."

"God Damn it! God damn worthless keepin' the consumer from his consumin' what's his God giv'n right to consume. More melancholy than John boy Walton when Thelma wouldn't kiss him 'cause of that mole on his face blue laws!"

John with only one pimple on his cheek didn't pop. He stared at the mist of rain droplets on the windshield. He opened his mouth to speak. The old man waited. "Want to keep going? There's a water fountain at the lake." He paused. "If you're thirsty."

"What! Drink the same stuff the fish pee in? Hardly!"

A raindrop splattered on the windshield. John would have absorbed all the water in the sky to keep the heavens from shedding some tears for a couple of hours. He sank in his seat.

"C'mon kid, don't get droopy on me." Don grinned his best W.C. Fields. "Ain't nothing pourin' here for a few hours. I guarantee ya Maryland Heights, St. Louis County, and the rest of Missouri is going to be bone dry till 11am this morning. We might as well go to the lake. Keep rollin'. Keep those cats from pourin.'" Don Murphy started singing the tune to the television series Rawhide.

And so the boy and the old man continued on their quest for the perfect fishing hole, just a mile down the road from Dirt Cheap Beer and Cigarettes.

CHAPTER 17

In this fishin' hole, the old man finds he hasn't lost his touch.

They descended. The slope down the hill was steeper than any the boy and the old man had encountered thus far on the their journey to the body of water they sought. The change in environment was as abrupt as the change in the gradient. Trees replaced houses as the primary occupant of the landscape. The truck nosed downward to match the slope of the road. The old man scratched his as he read the sign to the entrance of Creve Couer Lake Park.

"Not bad. Even smells different. Smells like the air fresheners at the supermarket. But better. Kid, what da ya think? Smells good ya?"

"Not bad. About the same. Smells the same as before."

Don breathed in the flora around him. Beneath the treetops, cut green grass, greener than the lawn in front of the houses previously passed, had given way to an array of ferns and wild flowering bushes. Clouds of vapor, puffy pillows of every shape and size, floated motionlessly, hovering like hummingbirds, above the bushes. The truck inched forward as Don absorbed the breathtaking beauty, preserved perfectly in time, before him. For a second, to the right, to the left, and in front of the truck this forest forever stood. The road pointed to a curve ahead. The truck followed the path. The forest gave way at its center, at its very heart.

John looked at the monolithic object was before them, lying horizontally, engrossing the view from within the confines of the cabin of his truck. The lake was colorless, bestowed the same gray by the sky above. There was no ripple on its surface, no texture whatsoever, a quality the foliage just passed possessed. A tone of dark green to a shade darker of gray was the only difference in his surroundings. Above the lake's surface was a dense fog, an impenetrable shroud, concealing the shores on the lake's far side. The sky, the water, the land bordering the lake looked the same to him. Lifeless. No one, except John O'Reilly and the Don Murphy, was in Creve Couer Lake Park this morning. The parking lot was empty.

"We fishin' on the pier over there?" The old man pointed at a dock twenty feet ahead extending endlessly into the lake. The fog was too dense to determine the length of the dock, or what purpose a sloping concrete road beside the dock could serve.

"I've fished off that pier. We could. There's a better place."

"Let's go to the better place, sort of creepy here, guy." Wisps of low lying fog, broken off from the main body over the lake, crawled about them. The leaves of trees about the lake whispered slightly in the wind imbuing the apparitions around Don with voices.

"Just fog. Cool morning. Warm water. Makes fog. There's a breeze. Won't last much longer."

"What's that?" Don scratched his arm. "Thatsa mosquito ain't it?"

"It's a lady bug."

"Damn right, it's a woman bug. Looks like it's tried to suck me dry! I'm welting. Where's the bug repellant, kid?"

"You won't need any where we're going."

"And just where are we going?"

"There's a cove on the other side of the lake."

"Well, if it's on the other side of the lake whatta we doin' parkin' of this side of the lake?"

"There's no road to where we are going."

"Kid, I'm too old to be walkin' around some lake ya can't see the other side of." Don pointed at a paved foot trail bordering the lake only, like the dock, to disappear into the fog."

"No foot trail, either."

"Kid, I don't know about you, but I know for a fact I can't walk on water. You might be able to do it, but I'm not gonna try it unless you got a pair of jet skis in the back of your pickup."

"There's a boat."

Don looked around him. No boat in sight. He gave the boy standing next to him a look in the head like the kind of doctor who guides his patient into the arms of two men holding a straight jacket. John did not sway from his statement. Don casually looked in the back of the truck expecting to find a pair of jet skis. There wasn't any. Just a tackle box, a lawn chair, and ten cane fishing poles.

John grabbed the tackle box and the fishing poles. His arms were full.

"Wait over by the boat ramp, I'll be there in a second." He tried to grab the lawn chair.

"I'll get the chair. You want me to wait over there next to the road going to nowhere?"

"Ya." John walked off into the fog.

Don sat down in the chair. In the distance he could hear something heavy being dragged. First, on grass, then on asphalt. The boy emerged from the fog with a rowboat behind him. Two oars, one on each side of the boat, skipped on the black asphalt. To Don, it appeared as if John was being aided by an unknown rower. John put the front of the boat in the water, stepped in, and grabbed the oars. His upper torso and the bow of the boat disappeared in the fog.

"Ok, let's go."

Don put a foot in the boat. "Wait. Wait. Wait. Charon. Excuse me headless rower of the river Styx takin' me to the far side of the Netherlands. You're just gonna row off with somebody's boat you don't own. Ya know, ya haven't payed for?"

"Boat doesn't belong to anyone. Not anymore."

"Huh?"

"It's broken. No one wants it. Worthless, I guess. I leave it over there in those bushes. Guess no one can see it. It's been here forever, since I started fishing here. No one messes with it. No one uses it except me."

"What da ya mean it's broken?"

"Got a crack in the stern."

113

Don took his foot out of the boat. "Listen here skipper of the U.S.S. Titanic, I'm not some dumb first mate. Don't do Disney World. Not gonna ride that Seven Thousand Leagues Under the Loch Ness ride. You're not taking me on some three hour tour endin' up with a walk on the bottom of the lake without any scuba gear are ya?"

"Ten minutes. Tops. It's a slow leak. I use that can to bail out the water." John lifted his arm through the fog and extended his finger at a rusted coffee can.

"Which side is the stern?"

"The back of the boat."

"I'll sit in the front. Sorry, can't help ya with the oarin'. Too old to hit some squid from deep down below over the head with an oar. All I can do is cheer ya on with a bird's eye from the surface. Sure ya know what you're doin?"

"Yes." The old man felt reassurance in this one syllable word. This was the first time he heard John's voice assume any assertiveness.

"All right kid. I'll get up in the crow's nest and keep a look out for icebergs. Crow's nest is a boat word. See, I know boat words, too. I's gots smarts like a professor do. Just checkin' ya."

The oarsman began to row. He rowed with no fear. The strokes were deliberate. The boat's edge cut into the soupy haze in jagged steps of time, slow, then fast, then slow again, matching the oarsman's pace of his staff between the two mediums, air and water, upon which no footing could be obtained, unlike land. The vessel's wake gave motion. Nothing else did.

"Reminds me of my last booze cruise, only on the way back. Hazy. Campbell could bottle this stuff and sell as soup ya can eat with a fork. How ya know where we goin', kid?"

"The cove's directly on the opposite side of the lake from the boat dock."

Don turned around. No curvature in the trail the boat made in the water. The waves feathered outward from the path like the end of an arrow. The craft rocked a bit as he got up to sit on the boat's tip. He took off his shoes, rolled up his pants, and dangled his toes in the water. He hummed the tune to Gillingan's Island, thirty seconds in length, examining his watch as if he were using the instrument to keep a beat, not tell time. He checked his metronome for the twentieth time.

"Land ahoy! Ahoy! Land! Boy, ya did it! Don Murphy splashed his feet in the water.

The faint outline of land was visible. The fog had taken shape. The images, hanging over the water's edge, formed. Trees, lined at land's end, clawed at the remains of the soil not eaten by the water's incessant erosion. Their roots, twisting one over another, formed a labyrinth of decaying wood stuck in soil the consistency of tar like sludge. The soup the ferryman and the passenger swallowed sickened their stomachs. The aroma of stagnate water permeated the air. Some of the tree roots appeared to unfurl. Creatures lacking limbs slid into the water as the ferryman's passenger, overjoyed to find land regardless of how hospitable this black beach was to his feet, splashed fervently in the same medium to which death's demons disappeared.

"Say kid. Turn around. What those slithering things?"

"Water snakes."

Don Murphy yanked his moccasins in the boat and counted his toes. This feat and putting his fingers not on his nose, but up his nose, he did quicker than a drunk, dried out from not having drunk any snake oil for twenty hours, can pass a police officer's sobriety test.

He sobbed, "Not gonna get swallowed by sea serpents. Ride over! I'm getting' off. Stop rowin', kid."

John stopped rowing. The water accumulating in the boat's stern continued forward. Don's feet got wet again.

"Don't stop rowin'. Keep rowin, kid! Wait! Peter give me that pan!" Don grabbed the coffee can. He scooped once. The land had a mouth, barely the boat's width, to engulf the water he bailed.

"This is the worst trip I've ever had. I've done cruised without booze and sunk to the bottom of hell. I'm too young for the netherworld. Disneyland. I wanna go to."

The boat continued onward, past the land on either side. The vessel pierced the fog. Light, diffused by the clouds above, illuminated from every direction holding the haze at bay. The gothic landscape astern was transformed into a serene sea of tranquility at the boat's bow. Butterflies, dancing in the air, partnered with John's tired steps of the oar, to tug the boat into the cove's port only yards ahead of the inlet's neck. Yellow flowers dripping with nectar lined the banks on either side of the cove. A narrow waterfall meandered from a fern filled cliff. The spout's output, cleansed crystal clear by the overflowing plant life miraculously thriving on nothing but barren rock and the light from above, did not permit the dark waters to penetrate past the entrance to this fisherman's paradise. The cove's bottom in plain view, too modest to be exposed, was completely covered by water grasses.

Don, stricken by one of nature's wonders, got around to completing his last thought. "Never.Never.Never mind. Never mind what I said, kid. Had faith in ya all along." He put his feet back in the water.

"Say kid, take a look at all these fishies in the water." Don wriggled his toes in the transparent liquid. Fish swam towards their realm's new visitor. "Hey kid, these things don't bite, do they?"

"Hope so."

The water was once again devoid of man's presence. The vessel struck ground at a harbor between two immense roots of an ancient oak tree. One nearly had to do an about face to see anything but a tree trunk directly ahead. The oak's bark was strong and scar free, no disease had weathered the wood's skin. Precisely perpendicular to the ground its roots anchored, the tree pointed straight to the heavens, over a hundred feet into the translucent medium above. The tree branches spread out to roof the cove, providing the birds above, and the fish underneath, with shelter. Its arms softly swayed, like the wands on the strings of an orchestra of violins, whenever the air grew restless. Any agitated soul would, upon listening, be lullabied to a sound slumber, to rest beside the cove's quiet waters. When the soul reawakened the leaves would whistle in the wind, echoing the song the birds played as they leapt beyond the boundaries of the branches and the world below. The tree, at the end of summer, was in the perfect state of growth. Then one leaf fell, an indication the inevitable was to come. One branch would soon be barren. Growth, to begin in the Spring anew, was soon to cease. The Fall was approaching.

Don picked up his lawn chair, and positioned it at the tree's base next to another lawn chair, an empty throne, waiting for an occupant.

"You leave this lawn chair here?"

"Always in the same place when I come back. No one fishes here but me." John sat down next to Don.

"Ok, kid. Let's get some. I'm hungry." He waited for the boy to move. John didn't respond. A minute went by. Then another. "Hey kid, doesn't look like you're gonna catch much by just starin' at 'em."

"Go ahead. Bait the hooks. Cast the lines. Fish 'ill do the rest." A minute went by. "I'm tired."

"Just one problem, what da ya mean by cast and lines, Captain Hook? I thought we fishin', not makin' a musical. I don't have a clue what ya talkin' about. You gonna have to learn me."

John lifted himself upright, reached into the boat, and grabbed the fishing poles. He turned over a rock with his foot to expose several worms wriggling in the rich soil underneath. He grabbed a handful and put the bait in the coffee can, which he held in the same hand as the tackle box. He did this with minimal energy, even as he juggled an arm full of poles underneath his armpit.

"Kid, look like you've got some practice at this."

117

"Here every Sunday. Sometimes Saturday. Good hole to go." Pause. "Good fishing." He handed a pole to Don. "First adjust how deep you want you're hook to go in the water. Go real deep and you'll catch catfish. Move the bob up a bit, you'll get a bass. I usually get perch or bluegill, when I put the bob close to the hook."

Don put his hands on the float. "Gotta a touch of the arthritis. Ya mind?"

"What kind of fish do you want to catch?"

"Kind that taste good fried. Put some distance between that mouse and the floaty. I wants me a catfish."

John grabbed a worm out of the can. "You want me to bait your hook?"

"Kid, closest thing I've come to stabbin' something still movin' was a thick slab of beef just shot in the rear of a Kansas City restaurant. Real juicy steak, rare, the way I like it. I'm fearful I might miss and prick myself. Wouldn't wanna poke my eye out and be branded a one-eyed worm eater for life. So the answer is yes."

"Can you cast?"

"Been a while, at least a decade, since I done some castin'. When was that?" Don shrugged his shoulders. "Oh well. Been so damn long I done forgit."

John tried to untangle the old man's response. "Can you toss the line out into the water?"

"Let me try, kid. What da ya know. Been a while, but I still got it in me. Kid, I tell ya what. You take care of the batin' part and I'll take care of throwin' out the lines. Hows that suit ya?"

"Ok." John baited all ten hooks. The old man tossed the lines, or better put, dropped the bob directly underneath the end of the pole. John propped the poles up against the tree root they sat upon.

Don helped. "Ok, kid. Don't get those lines crossed. Makes it easier to reel in the fishies that way."

The man and the boy sat down. John sat patiently. The old man fidgeted.

"What's happin' next, kid?"

"Wait for them to bite."

"When's that?"

John looked at the water. "Don't know. That's what makes it interesting." John looked at the old man. "Doesn't take long if they're hungry."

The old man looked around. He hummed. He twiddled his thumbs. He kicked his legs to and fro' rocking the lawn chair like a toddler in search of something to gain his attention. Don couldn't sit still.

"Yo guy, what are those yellow flowers bigger than roses from Texas over there?"

"Honeysuckles."

"Be back in a sec, kid." Don got up. Out of the corner of his eye, he saw one of the floats bobbing which was not the product of the ripples on the water's surface. Some character underneath was yanking on the line, with the finesse of a cat playing with a ball of yarn. Don spoke to his fellow hunter, not in a low cautious voice, but with excitement. He didn't care if the prey knew of the hunter's presence. "We got one! Reel in that fishy!"

"That's a nibble."

"How ya know that, kid? Bob, the worm stuck to a float, can't jump from Jaws like that."

"The cork will move like it's being sucked into a vacuum. Bite makes the pole flex more."

"Oh." He patted the boy on the shoulder. "Just makin' sure ya payin' attention."

Several minutes passed. Don squirmed, just like a worm trying to wriggle his way out of a can. John sensed the old man's attention deficit. He tried to think of something to say. Something to make the old man's fishing experience enjoyable.

"Fun, isn't it?"

"I don't know, kid. If we getta a mermaid, yes. If you land a whale, well. Tell ya what, why we're waiting for the fishies to start actin' up again, I'm gonna get a snack before the commercial break is finis."

Don defoliated an entire honeysuckle bush, using his shirt as a catch basin for the bush's petals in full bloom. He squeezed the sweetness from each flower, one after another. A trail of used stems sucked honey free followed his path to in front of his seat. A pile of litter, soon to be a junk yard of unsweetened tea dark leaves given his rate of consumption, accumulated next to his lawn chair.

"So whatdaya do beside fish here and stock over there at the grocery store, kid?"

"I work at Best Buy part time."

"Got my big screen TV at Asbestos Buy. One on Manchester Road. You sort of look like the sales dude who sold it to me."

"They hired me to sell computers there."

"You do sales?"

"My manager decided to use me to fill in for a computer technician who called in sick. They told me I should be a computer tech."

"What that?"

"I work on computers."

"Still don't get ya kid. That sentence ya spoke was a little too technical for me. Too brief for an old geyser like me, need a tad more output."

"When a customer has a problem with a computer they bought I try to fix it."

"Fix what? Give me a bit more info."

"The computer. Most of the time I can't fix the problem. I usually end up filling out paperwork and sending it to the service center for repairs."

"And? Still can't see, kid. Paint a picture for me. I know 'nough English to comprehend more than a couple of sentences at a time. I've been in that store few times. Never seen any computer tech heads before."

John spoke. Seconds went by between the words. Minutes between the sentences. While completely lacking patience for the fish to bite, nothing interfered with Don's focus on the individual beside him. Don took the time, every second of silence, every minute of voicelessness, to listen. A link formed between the listener and his subject.

"We're behind the sales counter where you check out. They converted some storage space next to where the defective merchandise is taken before it's shipped back to the manufacturer. Makes sense about what you said. I can see most of the store from where I'm at, but people have to practically stand at the computer repair counter to see anyone inside. I have to fill in for the security guard when they go to lunch. I answer the phone a lot. People call in with questions about how to use their computer. I try to help them out over the phone. They get frustrated when I tell them what to do. I guess it's because they're not looking at the same computer screen I am. Someone called. A few days back. I didn't understand what they were trying to tell me. When I asked them to repeat what they said. They hung up. Don't like that part of the job much."

"Well, it's 'bout time. 'Bout time I got a full paragraph out of ya. So why ya keep doin' it, kid?"

"Huh?"

The job, kid, why ya keep doin' the job if ya don't like it."

"I like it when I fix a customer's computer problem. That's fun. Used to do crossword puzzles when I was younger. It's like that when I solve one. Guess that's why I keep working there, even though I've been feeling well lately. That, and I need the money."

"If you don't feel good, you oughta do what I'd do. Take a few sick days."

"Don't get any sick days. Don't get paid if I call in sick. Need the money. Need to get my muffler on my truck replaced."

"No big deal kid. Just do what I do. Turn up the radio real loud. Put a muffle on that problem. Good way to fix the exhaust." He sung. "Cheap. Kinda shot ya can afford."

John didn't reply. He was exhausted from his verbiage, the longest conversation he had with anyone face to face in a month, even at work. His eyes focused on the floats in front of the two fishermen, closing, and reopening several seconds later, repeatedly. His crown resonated, tipping in unison with the flickering of his eyelids.

Don waited for the boy's eyes to reopen. "Kid, might be me, but I'd say you look a little worn out, like an 'ol jalopy I got in storage. You slouchin' over, look like you sittin' on empty. Ain't seeing no sparks twinklin' in those eyeballs of yours yearnin' to yank in some fishies, at all."

"I didn't sleep well last night. I haven't been sleeping well lately."

"Nope. Nope. Nope." Don put his hand on the boy's shoulder. "Don't take me for a dope, kid. You need more than just a tankful of gas to getcha goin'. Yous need a set of new plugs, maybe even an overhaul, 'fore ya even gonna spit out any smoke whatsoever from your chitty chitty bang bang."

John reawakened. The touch of a fellow fisherman willing to take the time to listen shook him. His lips quivered. His jaw trembled slightly. The muscles attached to his eyes strained in an effort to force his mouth to move to speak, exposing the veins surrounding his pupils, reddened from days of unrest. He exhaled, but no words came forth.

The old man smiled without exposing his teeth. Don peered into the boy's eyes and saw a reflection of his self in the youth's visual organ. In one phrase he had stripped away all but this one layer to the boy's gray matter. He would not pry further, he would not poke the boy in the eye. He gave comfort.

"So why ya come here so much kid?"

John breathed. His slouched figure reshaped. He put his elbow on his knee and his hand on his cheek. He molded a thought. "I like it here. No worries. Always able to rest here with no problem. I can dream here. Get filled up with." He turned to look at Don for a word.

"I understands ya, kid. Keep on goin'."

"I do my best thinking here. Haven't had to many ideas, lately though. Only thing I've been thinking of." He paused. "Is one question. What else is there?"

"Kid, when you ponder that question yous got yourself one real big problem. But I think I knows what ya need. A solution to your dilemma." The old man stood up and pointed both his right and left index finger at the boy.

"Our philosophic grandfathers, all the way back to Plato and Aristotle, have pondered the exact same question for day's on end to no avail." Don pointed his left hand down and the right hand up to make his philosophical point, then he pointed at himself. "I's got the perfect answer. A solution to what's troublin' ya. The answer me and a few great men before me have discovered is so simple yet elegant once ya know it you'll be countin' fluffy sheepies all night long. Ya know what it is?"

"No. What is it?"

"YOU GOTTA GET LAID!"

The boy pondered over Don's statement.

"Kid, ya know, make some bacon with Betty for breakfast 'cause ya gotta a hog in yo' crock pot. Ya gotta do the hanky panky 'cause ya gotta a puss knockin' yo' boots. Howl at the moon 'cause the sheep dog just left ya alone to guard a pasture full of little lambs. Put some cream in Swiss Miss's cocoa 'cause she wants to yodel on yo' love ukulele. Hang like Tarzan from the chandeliers 'cause Jane wants to swing from yo' love monkey. Jack, ya gotta do some jumpin' for joy in the bed with Jill 'cause she's slippin' in yo' sheets. You need to do some beastin' with two backs in the sack 'cause Sally wants to slap yo' sex snake. Ralph, ya gotta get get off yo' heals 'cause ya gotta a bone yous gonna hide between Heidi's hips."

He reached out to poke the boy on the shoulder with his index finger. "You need to sleep with a woman that's got some big fluffy pillows!"

Don stood in the boat, placing one foot on top of the bow. He poised for a portrait, a side profile from John's point of view, with all the grandeur of Washington crossing the Delaware.

"I have done it over 25,000 times. 27,320 times to be exact. And not a once did I fail to sleep like a baby afterwards." He eyed the boy. "Kid, I can tell by the way your jaw just dropped, you are in complete and total awe at my incredible accomplishment. Who wouldn't be? Let ya in on a little secret. Don't tell this to hardly anyone. Can't hardly believe it myself. At times I'm a little overcome with emotion at the amount of sexual fornication I have created through the years. A history over five decades in the making, a span lasting over forty years, forty seven years fives months, and."

"What's the time, kid?"

"I don't know." The boy was still working on an answer to the meaning of life.

Don knew the answer on the process to producing life, down to the science of statistics calculated to precision given the date. He looked to the sky as Ptolemy, the medieval astronomer, would searching for the Sun. Without a sundial, he resorted to the watch on his wrist.

"A span of forty seven years five months. And in another five hours ten minutes and thirty two seconds, Lord willin' ya can row us thru the gates of hell past them Medusa snakes hissin' like Ulysses sirens and doublin' up as Madonna's funky new haircut back to safety on the opposite side of this here lake straight out of the Twilight Zone, it'll be seven days.

John looked at the old man bobbing in the boat no differently than he did the other floats in the water.

"Ok, kid. I can tell. I know what ya thinkin'. Ya thinkin' 'so what.' Big deal when everyone knows Walt Chamberlain had a well-documented career achievement of dunking his hoola in over 20,000 different cheerleader's hoops, and here it is I've only scored 27,320 times. That means I would have to have nearly a one on one ratio of game to score to compare. I admit it! I'm not even close to six one. But I've gone for quality, which makes me better. I have assisted precisely 2,732 woman to soar to new heights, feet up in the air, backs horizontal, bouncin' off my headboard as I dunked them into ecstasy's greatest basket of 'em all, the sexual orgasm. Now 27,320 times divided by 2,732 women is 10, and as everyone knows, no one can outdo a perfect 10, only tie it. When ya take into account my stature's not even close to Wilt the stilt, actually, that's an advantage, makes my donger look longer. Never mind that one. But when ya consider for fifteen uninterrupted years I had the breakfast of champions every morning and always had dessert, never a helpin' from the same cherry pie mo' than five days in a row, I'm the best there has, is, or ever will be. My statue is destined to replace Casanova standin' behind Cleopatra in the Wax Museum of Love in Times Square. Might even get a star on the side walk with my name engraved in gold in the Red Light district over there in Amsterdam, too."

As a result of the future Sex Hall of Famer's wild arm waving the boat had broken anchor. Don grasped at the closest fishing pole in an attempt to re dock. He then grabbed his pole and steadied himself, hollering into the small oasis before him, "I am Don Juan Domingo, the greatest lover of them all!"

Instantaneously the float attached to the fishing pole Don held dived deep into the water making the cane pole arc to the point of snapping. The old man held on, mustering every ounce of strength in his faded body. This skilled hunter wasn't letting a swashbuckling swordfish of the Caribbean break from his clutches let alone some worm snatcher from this cozy little cove. The pole, energy stored in it's flexion, rebounded, extending once again to it's previous state of stiffness. A catfish leaped out of the water into the boat, flopping helplessly out of control at its captor's feet.

"Yes. Yes. Yes. Didn't doubt for a second. Still got it in me. Haven't lost my touch!" The old man groped for the fish. "It's too slippery. Whoa! Damn thing gones on the attack! Kid, I need your help! I'm stuck in a boat takin' in water with a fish madder than Moby Dick!"

The boy grabbed the line, lifting the catch into the air. The fish floundered, jostling against the air's invisible resistance briefly, before succumbing to exhaustion. Escape to the whiskered feline fish's former resting spot on a bed of grass covering the cove's bottom was futile. The nabbed cat hooked on a string continued to strain relentlessly to catch its breath, sucking wind through lungs not designed to obtain oxygen from air.

"Hold onto it while I get the net."

"Good show, kid. Looks like she willin' to pucker up, call by gones by gones. Ha! Too late! She ain't getting' off the hook that eazie. She gonna make me some supper first. Then we'll see if she up to talkin' after that. I gotta good feelin' the only feedback I'll be givin' is some after dinin' belchin'." The line swung toward Don. He got a whiff of his tied captive. "Sure 'nough. Smells like the real thing a little on the sour side."

John went to the base of the old oak tree. He returned with a net, lying in the same location he left it from his previous excursion to the cove. The old man was about to put the captive in the cage made from string, but refrained from handing his catch over to the boy. He pointed at the fish's lungs.

"What that in the fishie's mouth?"

"Looks like a piece of leather. People throw a lot of garbage in the lake. Catfish are bottom feeders."

"Damn right they're bottom feeders! This one done ate some poor chap all the down to his wallet. That's all that's left. Be careful when you let this one lose in that net of yours. This one's a man eater!"

No sooner had the boy removed the hook from the catfish, tying the net in the partially submerged boat to give the fish some reprieve in the medium it could catch its breath, was the old man holding onto his pole with all his strength to reel in another hostage. Again the boy unhooked the fish, a scrappy bluegill, allowing the catch to regain its dignity as best it could in a net with an inhospitable neighbor, the worn out catfish. Don touched two new poles, and in so doing a fat bass and a wiry perch not even thick enough to make a meal for a winged fisherman above were added to the collection. The old man didn't care what he caught just that he caught something. Each fish was the object of his attention only as long as it remained hooked. Once netted, he yanked on his pole again without hesitation, indifferent to the precise nature of the not manlike lunged creature he last subdued. The cycle repeated so rapidly fish appeared to jump clear out of the water chasing Don's lure into the center of the net making a swooshing noise as they landed. The netted fish, all ten caught in less than a minute, did not become the best of companions. The bass didn't hit it off with perch, but the perch did hit the bass with a fin. The bass had a large mouth and bellowed back, biting the perch in the tail which jumped causing the catfish to paw the bluegill. In return, the bluegill punched the catfish with its dorsal arm until the cat's belly was black and blue.

"See what happens kid, when ya get too many egg layers cooped in the same hen house."

The old man leaned over John's shoulder as the boy tried the best he could to control the commotion in the sack he held, ready to hatch into epic disproportions unless he could adeptly create some slack. Don knew how to enlarge his captive's holding cell.

"Just let them swim around in the boat. Makes a good fishy bowl. Ain't no tide gonna let them out. Yes! Got my Midas touch back! Haven't done associations like that in a long, long, time. Hold that thought, kid. I got to do some business in the bushes. Can't control it like I used to."

The tidy bowl man disappeared into the bushes behind the oak tree. John scooped Don's trophies back into the net, a child's catch the second time around given the size of the basin they swam in.

"I feel relieved. Haven't felt this cushioned since I ran into a door with a harem on the other side of it in Tehran, Iran back in '79. Better than that! I been rejuvenated!" The old man started dancing and singing.

"Caught a fish, caught a fish,
What a dish, what a dish.

Don't tell my ex wife, once my wife,
I'm living up life, living up life.

127

If you did, if you did,
I would have to set sail, set sail,
Or get booted big time in the tail, in the tail.

If this fish could speak, could speak.
She would have said, would have said.
Tell his wife so he too will lose his head, lose his head.

As I was stuffin' fishies in my pocket, had to go, had to go.
Took a whiz, did my biz, at a mill on that hill, that hill.

Saw the game warden not named Bill,
Oh was she big, big Jill, big fat Jill.
She whipped out a ruler as I tried to slip it in my pants, slip it in my pants.
She said, "That one's not in regulation. Put it back in, put it back in!"

"Pretty good jingle I just invented, ya?"

"You just made that up? How'd you do that?"

"Good with words. That's why I'm a writer. Oh it's been awhile, let me tell ya, but I think I'm passin' through 'the block.'"

"The block?"

"That's what us writers get when we can't think of nothin' to whittle on paper. Terrible affliction to get. Terrible. Oh, how have I had 'the block.'" Don moaned. "But, I'm movin' 'gain! Must have been that bottle of Ex-Lax I swallowed last night. I'm just bullshittin' ya, kid! Ripley, believe it or not its 'cause ya helped' me out with my problem." He patted the boy on the shoulder. "Sos I want to help ya out with yours. Ya in the single digits aren't ya, guy?"

John was depressed. He wasn't dumb. He had no doubt in his mind what the old man's references regarded. As he thought of providing a verbal answer, he slouched, and with each exhale further contorted his body to a sunken state. He spoke without a breath.

"Yes."

"I tell ya what. Make a deal with ya. You honest with me. I be up front with you. I tell ya the truth why I stuck so with my pen. Way back when the ink was flowin' wild on paper I was doodlin' nonstop on naked women with the pen I kept on me all the time, too. Ya know, the pen I kept in my pants even when I wore pants with no pockets. Now I can't tell ya how long it's been since I has drawn a picture of an unclothed lady. I don't divulge in matters personal about myself like that. But,I think yous can help me remember where I misplaced my pen in my old age, Ponce de Leon."

John took a second to comprehend the old man's reference to the famed Spanish explorer who sought the fabled Fountain of Youth.

"Kid, if ya don't understand me, let me know. Listen to this here deal too good to pass up. Me and you, we go huntin' together round town. You provide the gimmick while I'll do the grabbin'. I gets to hook 'em first since I got all the experience, of course, but yous learn by watchin' and before yous know it ya be a master just like me."

John just looked.

"Okay. Okay. Okay. I be damned I never had to stoop so low before. I'll take the sloppy seconds. Ya can go first. What da ya say?"

Several thoughts swam in Johns' head. That the old man was a writer was plausible. He recalled his first meeting the old man at the supermarket in the paperback aisle. The old man had volumes of books in his apartment also, further adding credibility to his being an author. As to the subject of Don's books, John could only fathom as to the depth of Don's discourse, even though clues abounded. Donald Darren Murphy or Don Juan Domingo, whatever the old man's name was, more than likely Don Murphy, was articulate at times. Don also slurred his speech occasionally. He had an uncontrollable desire to drink as John witnessed at the trash dumpster, but only for a certain type of alcoholic beverage, not the type John almost drank at the old man's apartment. John didn't know what to think. The last thing the old man said to him about not knowing, not understanding, blended with John's inability to accurately characterize Donald Darren Murphy. This thought jumped from his head.

"I don't know."

The old man caught the thought and worked with it. "That's close enough to yes. We gotta a verbal handshake, we do a real one and we has got ourselves a done deal."

John looked at the garden before him. He didn't extend his hand to match the old man's.

"Awe, c'mon on kid. Don't look at me like that. You look like you getting' a bum deal."

John stood up. "We've caught some. I'm ready to go whenever you are. I don't feel like fishing anymore."

"Ya not upset with me just 'cause I caught all the fish? Can I help if I'm a great angler able to catch any dish even it's the first time dippin' my pole in this here waterin' hole. See, it's just 'cause I've got a great lover's name. That's all. You just gotta try, kid. Ya still got some fishin' in ya. I can tell."

John grabbed the nearest pole partially to appease the old man, but Don was correct. The boy's will to catch one on his own was depleted, but the desire to do so was as firmly rooted as the tree he stood upon. Don provided the encouragement the boy needed to regain his will.

"That's right. Just do it. Ya don't need no bait. Angle with a silver hook."

John cast a naked line far into the cove, near the waterfall's spout, encased by an arch hued with only one color, gold, given from the soft glowing light above. There was immediate tension in his staff. The line became taut. John, using one last ember of willpower residing in his body, coerced the bitten, wearing a shiny ringed ornament, from the water. He almost jumped out of his shoes, as the beautifully scaled creature, a rainbow trout in full prime, yanked back on the line luring the boy into the water with a tail's splash. But alas, as all men have feet, John was not withdrawing to the water to chase mermaids. With one last stand, holding his pole one handed, he convinced the trout to join him on the dry land, not that the trout was about to let John walk freely. He was entangled in line, wrapped several times about his body, but in particular, around the finger between his little finger and middle finger on his left hand the most. John had been ringed, too.

"What did I tell ya, kid. Good catch, too. See what a little luck can do for ya. Now as I was sayin' about our deal."

The heavens opened. The clouds released. The rain began to fall. Neither fisherman doubted soon the air would be saturated, having the same weight and density as the liquid the lake contained.

"This air is gonna get so thick we gonna need gills to breathe it. I'm too old to get wet, kid. I'll melt."

John looked up. "There's a break in the clouds. I can make it. We'll get soaked for sure if we stay here." He heaved water from the boat with the rusted coffee can as quickly, being covered in tangle, as he could.

The old man, upon seeing the boy's predetermination to leave the cove immediately, grabbed the coffee can. "I believe in ya. I think ya can make it before it starts to pour. I'll take care of the bailin' us out part."

John, faster than a reporter can jump into a telephone booth to call in a news line, untwined from the threads wrapped around him. He leaped into the boat jumping clear over the tree root upon which previously he sat stumped. Like a locomotive's wheels beginning to roll, his oars pushed slowly, spinning great vortexes of water towards the traveler bailing water behind him. With each stroke he gained more speed, steaming ahead faster than a sailboat on Creve Coeur Lake.

"Great Scott! You've put some distance between us and that cove." Between bails, Don Murphy took guard not to let any of his catch in the net escape to the lake, including the trout attached to John's fishing pole. He turned to face the boy upon hearing thunder ahead. "Zeus is hurlin' bolts of fire from the sky! Heave ho, kid. Don't stop rowin' for nothin'!"

Don caught a glimpse of his oarsman in full gallop. His stoker's engine was running red hot. Sweat glistened on the boy's forearms and shoulders. Two years of continually stocking shelves and lifting crates of produce all day while eating a diet of toasted oats at night had produced results. His muscles were lean and as well striated as any stallion. He was not overburdened with muscle, but the muscle he had was conditioned to making long untiring strokes of his oar as best any rower of Olympian stature. A few drops of rain combined with some beads of hard work made John's T-shirt cling to his stomach. There was a six pack a few feet in front of Don Murphy. The old man had no inclination for beer, instead, sticking his tongue out to taste a few drops of rainwater.

"Row Popeye, row. Thirty forty feet an' we there. From the way you rowin' this here can couldn't have been filled with coffee, had to been spinach."

John's boat struck land, skidding onto the dock whence the fishermen had departed. He unhooked his trout, guiding the fish gently back in the water.

"What ya doin'! That was a keeper for sure. Would have made a great meal and some leftovers, too."

"Caught it once. Maybe some day, I'll catch it again." John looked at Don's netted fish.

"No way. They free here. Cost ya an arm an' a leg if ya go get 'em at the supermarket. I'm keepin' all of 'em."

No sooner had Don set foot inside the cabin of the boy's truck, did the deluge begin. Fish flopped around in the back of the boy's pickup bed with Don taking a peek now and then to watch the festivities. The old man licked his lips all the way home.

He whistled the tune to Snow White and the Seven Dwarfs, "Hi ho, Hi ho," thinking to himself, "I don't recall Droopy being able to row a boat like that, or Mopey, either. You think too much to be Dopey. I can't make ya out, kid. But I will."

The boy joined in, whistling along. He had to go to work tomorrow, Monday. Labor Day was a busy day at Best Buy. Today, on Sunday, he had gathered strength to endure another week.

CHAPTER 18

Who's Bernie?

"Before we do some belchin'," the elder John motioned the junior John towards their home's entrance, "let's step into the study for a minute."

John Jr. suddenly felt his stomach shake. "I don't feel so good, Dad. I'm gonna go lie in bed for awhile."

"No problem. Lie down on the couch in my study."

"Dad, I feel sick. My belly's really startin' to ache."

"I've even got a bottle of antacids in my desk drawer in the study to slow your tummy down."

The two stepped into John's den, the elder opening the door for the younger. The wall opposite the door was hidden behind a layer of computers, computer monitors, computer peripherals, computer software, computer accessories and paraphernalia.

Over thirty computers, some stacked four high, lined the floor at the wall's base. The number varied given the computing instruments O'Reilly needed at the moment, as such most of the computers were on rolling platforms in order to enhance mobility. The computers not on platforms were his workhorses, the machines he used to do most of his work. Of these, his most recent purchase, made fifteen months ago, was his favorite. Boncoeur's new technology had produced the most powerful personal computer, clocked at 700 Ghz, to date, until last week. Boncoeur's newest microprocessor, using light instead of transistors, was the first to surpass the Thz barrier. O'Reilly wanted one, but so far he had resisted the temptation. He preferred to purchase slightly older technology in bulk at a much more economical price.

The 700 Ghz computer came with a 60-inch flat screen monitor. The big screen monitor allowed gave him the ability to see the output from dozens of programs running simultaneously. Fifteen monitors, attached to swiveling bases mounted to the wall, flanked both sides of the main monitor. Any of the thirty computers could be attached to any monitor at the push of a button. More monitors with bigger screens were not necessarily better. O'Reilly could see more, and with better clarity, from a pair of goggles. BoncoeurVision outputted 3-D images so realistic the human eye could not perceive a difference between the Pebble Beach golf course in Florida and the holograms made by this visual imaging apparatus.

A counter, the length of the wall, functioned as a work desk. Between stacks of closed books, twenty-five books in various stages of being read were spread open. Five were near completion, ten were somewhere in the middle, and five were stuck on the first page. Every book on the counter pertained to some facet of computer science. A pile of fifty books, the tallest pulp skyscraper of the lot with a paperback foundation and a hardcover penthouse, stood precariously like a house of cards ready to tumble at the slightest touch.

Rows of shelves, one on each end of the desk to cover the wall where the monitors did not, climbed like a ladder to the ceiling. On the left side, each row contained Compact Disk after Compact Disk. On the right side, each row contained Optical Disk after Optical Disk. Every disk on each shelf contained information pertaining to computers. Either the disk's information was to enhance a person's computer knowledge, an electronic book, or the information was to enhance a computer's functionality, a computer program. Each was useless without the other, but when a user's computer operating know how combined with a computer running a properly operating program, the result was an enhancement in productivity by a billion. O'Reilly and one properly programmed computer could do the work of a thousand million computerless men.

O'Reilly did all his work at home at this desk. A craftsman had built the desk, with one row of drawers underneath the desktop, and a bookcase, built into the room's left wall upon entering the study, to O'Reilly's specifications. O'Reilly got the room and the custom carpentry when he made an agreement with his wife to keep all his techie toys, what she called his computer stuff, out of the kitchen.

Computer books lined every shelf of the bookcase except the lowest shelf. On this shelf were his wife's veterinary science textbooks and a variety of novels. Rarely did O'Reilly open the books on the bottom shelf. Occasionally, he would open an anthology of Milton as a sleeping aid. In a matter of minutes he was snoring on the study's old leather couch beneath the window with a view to the front yard.

The room's wall to wall carpeting had been replaced by oak flooring. Fringed on all corners by wood, a Persian rug of intricate detail, originally the King of Saudi Arabia's so the story went as told by one of the rug's former holders, occupied the study's center. The ruggedness of the carpet's craftsmanship was unparalleled by any other flooring. In sixteen years of continual use only a single thread had unraveled. Otherwise, Aladdin's flying carpet was in mint condition, and worth a mint, too.

"You should listen to your mother and not eat so quick," John Sr. closed the study door. "Your mother told me she felt nauseated after she took a look at your report card."

John Jr. sat on the couch. John Sr. rolled his office chair towards the couch.

"What grades did you bring home?" John Sr. put on his reading glasses to inspect the list of letters on the last column of the report card. "Let's start in the middle. How did you manage a C in Physical Education?"

"You get graded on whether you show up on time. I've been late a few times."

"And you haven't skipped your last class of the day, P.E., a few times have you?"

Junior didn't reply.

"So you can make it to your last class on time if you don't spend your afternoons at my office hanging out with my associates?"

"Ya."

"OK. What else do we have here? B+ in your computer sciences class?" O'Reilly thought to himself, "My boy got a B+ in programming? You're kiddin' me."

John Jr. frowned, "I turned in a program for a test last week coded in J++, but the teacher wanted it done in C++ so I got a D+."

"Did the program work right?"

"Ya."

"OK. No big deal, even if you get a final grade of B in the class."

Pound. Pound. Pound. Thump. Thump. Thump. Someone was knocking on the door.

"Daddy, what are you guys doin' in there?"

"Kathy, I'm talking with your brother. Give us a minute."

"Daddy, would you come out and play with me and my dollies?"

"In a minute, Kathy."

A distracted John Jr. stood up.

"Not so quick, Speedy Gonzalez. Take a Tums and have a seat. Here we go. Here's a good one. An A+ in your mathematics class. And what's this? Your teacher wrote a note on the report card?" O'Reilly read aloud, " John shows exceptional ability in mathematics. He consistently helps fellow students solve their advanced calculus problems."

Junior smiled.

"Ya know ya get your math skills from me," John Sr. boasted. "I was good at calculus in college, too."

"I'm doing partial differential equations. It's harder than calculus."

"Oh. Ok, tell me why ya can make an A in math and you're gettin' a D in biology? Why the difference?"

"I don't like biology. It's boring. I don't want to be a biologist. I want to program computers like you taught me, Dad. I don't need to know anything about biology."

"What if you get hired by a pharmaceutical company and in order to write one line of one program you have to know something about how a heart pumps? Huh?"

"I don't want to work for a drug company. I want to work with you, Dad."

"Listen, to me," O'Reilly opened his eyes wide. He wanted his son to open his eyes, too. "Smart people can learn anything from anyone. That's why they're smart. One source of information makes you one-dimensional. You're going to live in a small world, only able to see things one way, if you look at it with only one eye. You're going to be square if you're one-dimensional."

"Actually, Dad."

"Ok, Einstein. You can't even be a box if you're one-dimensional. Understand?"

"Ya."

"You've got to know a little about everything before you can know a lot about anything. You might find out you like biology if ya put a little effort into learning it so why don't you spend a little less time in math and get that grade in biology up to a C."

"Ok."

"Tell me how someone who can write computer programs in twenty different languages is getting a one legged A in their English composition class?"

"I'm really surprised I got an F, Dad."

"Why?"

"I thought I was doing much worse. The best grade I've made in the class is an H, but that's pretty good compared to the guy sitting in the back of the class."

"Why's that?"

"He's making Z's." Junior looked at Senior' face. "I'm not joking, Dad. Most everyone gets S's to M's on their homework. I heard someone got a D on a paper one time. I think that's been the best grade so far."

"So what you're telling me is your English teacher is going to flunk everyone or give everyone except the guy sleeping in the back of class a final grade of C?"

"Ya."

Pound. Pound. Pound. Thump. Thump. Kathy was knocking on the door to the study.

"Kathy, I'm busy! I can't play right now."

Kathy O'Reilly began to cry. Between sobs John Sr. and John Jr. listened to a young girl whine about not gaining entrance to where the boy's played.

"Mommy, Daddy doesn't want to play dollies with me." Kathy cried. "But Mommy, you were standing at the door. Why can't I?"

The younger John stood up, disgusted with the commotion created from his being the center of attention.

"I want my goggles back."

"Awe c'mon, Dad."

"When you get your biology and writing grades up, you can have 'em back. Understood?"

"Ya." John Jr. paused at the doorway so his mother and sister could make way for his exit.

"Dad, I'm going over to Bernie's."

"Who's Bernie?" replied his mother.

"Someone in my class." Junior walked out the house's front door.

"Daddy would you come play Barbie with me?"

The father didn't reply to his daughter. He was focused on the books on the bottommost shelf of the bookcase.

"Mommy will play Barbie with you for a little while."

John O'Reilly cautiously took his eyes away from the bookshelf. His daughter was gone.

"If she can zip through the phone book blindfolded."

He didn't waste a moment more. He vaulted every book on the bottom shelf over the topmost shelf. With the books well out of reach, and view, of his daughter's investigating fingers, he inspected the title of each book. Some he moved, such as his wife's biology textbooks, back to the bottom shelf. Others he did not.

"X is for Ecstasy. Definitely stayin' on the top shelf. L.A. Hitcher Hiking to Las Vegas by Alberta Kitchencock. No way. The Arabian who flew over Lawrence, Kansas. Kinda of interesting. Nope. Fiddler on the Babylon Roof. Hmmm. Well. Absolutely not. She Said Her Name Was Barb He Said His Name Was Ken. How bad can that one be?"

Mrs. O'Reilly's husband read one page, then another. Before he knew what got in him he was on the tenth page. Would his wife want to play dolly with him? He certainly was in the mood to play Barbie with her, but not the way Ken played in the backyard sandbox. Then again, groping for a couple of his wife's seashells in the sandbox sounded like a lot fun right now.

CHAPTER 19

Doctor, doctor give me the news, I got a bad case of…

John labored all day Labor Day at Best Buy. He spent his time watching others walk by with newly purchased computers while he stood within the room formerly occupied by unwanted merchandise. Other than wasting the afternoon in a vain attempt to recover data from a customer's hard drive, the day was uneventful. He was tired when he opened the door to his apartment in the evening.

Lately, he walked past the answering machine on the table near the kitchenette without even taking the slightest glance at the device. No one ever called. The last message he had received was from the office manager at the doctor's office to remind him of his appointment the next day with Bill Mueller, the therapist. Two weeks later, the answering machine's light was again blinking once intermittently. A single message had been left. John didn't need to be reminded of his appointment tomorrow. He put a finger on the machine's erase button, but the hope someone desired to speak with him made him push the replay button.

The relays on the magnetic reader of John's antiquated answering machine clicked. The reader's contacts touched magnetic tape. The device squeaked, "Hi. This is John. I can't come to the phone. Please leave a message."

The message followed, "Ohhhh. Ohhhhh. How my belly aches. Overindulged in those honey flower things. Ohhhh. Need 'yo help, kid. Come on over when ya gots the time."

Something was fishy about the old man's voice. He'd taken on an even deeper Southern pitch. He spoke as if he were from the backwoods of Louisiana, but he didn't sound ill. John hurried over to the old man's apartment anyway. The old man opened the door. An aroma greeted John. A very fowl odor flew through the air.

"What took ya so long, kid?"

"Just got home from Best Buy."

What ya lookin' at me like that for?"

"Your apartment smells. Really bad. Like fish."

"Really? Can't smell a damn thing. Nose clogged up. Thought 'bout puttin' the fishies in the bird bath bowl in the backyard but that'd be cruel and unusual punishment. Birds wouldn't have nothin' to drink from. So I did the next best thing I could think of. The fishies is swimmin' in my sink. They's happy 'cause I've invited them to supper. Just one problem."

The old man motioned for the boy to follow him to the kitchen. The boy got a look at the old man's apartment. Hundreds of compact disks were scattered on the floor next to the table held up by the four naked ladies. Next to the table was a wall full of stereo equipment. The stereo components were, both in number and variety, comparable to the most expensive sound equipment sold at Best Buy.

"Went to get some stuff out of storage today. Had to leave the jukebox behind. Ain't 'nough space in this here apartment the size of a shed."

A three-foot stack of paper adjacent to the old man's ancient typewriter provided the source for a flood of sheets spilling onto the tabletop. Paper sprinkled the floor, the result of any overflow from the table. The bookcase was barren. Books littered the floor. The coffee table supported the rest of Don's literary pieces on a tablecloth of naked ladies. The naked figures in the Playboy magazine John stared at yesterday hadn't moved an inch. John took a step into Dirty Don's pigpen. The old man cleared a path for the two kitchen seekers by kicking books out of the way.

"Gettin' started writin' on my next best seller. What us writers call 'work in progress.'"

The smell of fish became more pungent with each step toward the kitchen. John's nose clogged. His eyes winced. Ten fish were floating belly up in the kitchen sink.

"I was 'bout ready to skin 'em this morning, but turns out I was in for a bad arthritis day. Would ya mind, kid? I pay ya ta get 'em stripped for me. Name yo' price 'cept not too much. Only gots a little change on me."

"You don't have to pay me." John started skinning two weeks worth of weekday suppers for the elderly gentleman a few spokes short of a straight rim and maybe in need of Meals on Wheels.

"You told me yesterday, you not makin' 'nough money to buy no muffler. Now ya turnin' away cash. Which is it? You rich or poor, kid?"

"I get enough to eat." John scraped on the last fish. The scrawny perch would make a meager meal. "I'll take this one home as payment."

"How much money ya make from those two jobs of yours, anyway?"

"I made $17,000 last year," the boy replied with as much pride as a sharecropper can produce when buying an apple at the market, the profit from the fruit of his labors after the landlord had taken his share.

"My God. How da ya survive? My motel bill alone from last year was $17,000."

"I make enough. Even been saving money. A hundred more dollars and I'll have enough saved to get the parts for a computer I'm going to put together. Been saving almost a year."

"What? You gonna make a computer? You nuts. Ya need one of 'em factories over in Indonesia to do that. That's where my computer come from."

"Most computer parts are manufactured in East Asia. Taiwan, Singapore, for instance," the boy spoke with some authority. "But the parts can be assembled into a computer anywhere. Like an automobile. How do you know yours was make in Indonesia?"

"That's what Dell told me! I called up Dell's 800 number. Waited an hour. Told 'em I need help. They told me to call Microsofty. Waited two hours to tell Bill Microbates my problem. One his serfs said it was too hard, then they kept sayin' 'where?' I told 'em I got the Intel inside my dining room an' it ain't cookin'. They said call Intel so I could get some gal named Ethel's address. Waited three hours to talk to some unintelligent moron at Intel. Said to him, 'All I want to do is connected to the world wide net.' He said, 'Are you on a network?' Now how the hell do I suppose ta know if the net works? I never been tied up in no elect tronic net before. Not that I haven't never been tied up. I have. So I sais, 'Yes, the network works.' Didn't want to sound stupid or nothin'. Mr. Unintel says back, 'Dell uses 3Com. Call 'em. They know Ether's address.' Guess that's Ethel's sister. Anyway, that's when I found out my computer's home address is Indonesian. I swear that 900 number I sat on hold for four hours is gonna get billed to 3Com. I talked to some chick from China who could only speak a few letters of English and numbers. For ten whole minutes she kept sayin' the same thing over and over 'gain. Ya know computers. Can you make heads or tails of this?"

The old man handed John a piece of paper with twelve characters, 00C04F2C094F, scribbled repeatedly. Don Murphy had written down his computer's network interface card's Ethernet address, the address his computer used to send and receive information over the information superhighway, the Internet, multiple times.

John put on his computer repairman face, a look of inquisition for a puzzle ready to be pried into a solution. The old man pointed at the Dell computer sitting in the dining room corner, currently being used as a shelf for reams of paper.

"Got a pile load of paper on sale at the Office Depot. Gonna need it. Gots lots of writin' to do."

The Dell was top of the line, containing the fastest Intel microprocessor available, a Pentium II 400 mHz. With a 10 GB SCSI hard drive Don's PC was currently being used as a paper tray, nevertheless, the Dell was capable of functioning as a network server, providing other computers with tons of information. An inspection of the back of the computer's case revealed the box came fully loaded. Nothing could match the whistle made by this PC's SoundBlaster Awe32 soundcard when a pretty girl walked by. A 28.8 bps U.S. Modem could send her a love letter via e-mail in a heartbeat. The Matrox 3-D video card could even paint a pretty bouquet of flowers so realistic she wouldn't know the difference between a real rose and the electronic version seen on the 17 inch monitor planted next to the computer. Except for the smell; however, a verbal description of the rose's scent could be attached as a sound file to a love e-mail along with the rose's picture by means of the PC's Snappy audio-video to digital device. With his first look, John fell in love with the computer on site.

The answer was apparent to his discerning eye. Don Murphy, entering his golden years, had attempted to enter the Age of Information by inserting the end of his phone line into the network interface card manufactured in Indonesia by 3Com.

Don peered over the boy shoulder. The backseat driver swore, "Damn thing don't do nothing but show windows! I ain't doin' no cleanin'. That's what the maid for. Made in America my ass. Good thing I paid with plastic for this damn Japanese junk."

John plugged the phone line into the computer's modem. He checked the end of the phone cord to ensure it was connected to the phone jack. John had Don's Dell computer plugged into the Internet in thirty seconds flat. In another thirty seconds he had Netscape's Navigator Internet Web Browser zooming on Nascar's official web site. He clicked the mouse button as Don pointed on the screen where to go next.

"Ya done it. Ya fixed my computer!" Don Murphy witnessed, for the first time, the slimmest of something similar to a smile on the boy's face.

"You just put the phone line into the wrong connection."

"No way. It's a miracle! I spent all damn day getting' this damn computin' thing to do what ya did in a minute. You a miracle worker. I owe ya a million."

Don had blown a few breaths of life supporting words into the boy's ears. Freud's organ between John's ears was until now completely deflated. "I've been trying to get a full time position as a electronic service technician at Best Buy's repair service center." As the words came from John's mouth his brain deflated, "But they said I don't know enough yet."

"Well they a bunch of idiots workin' there. They can't fix a TV worth a shit." Don pointed at his big screen TV.

"I'm trying to learn how to fix a TV. That's what the repair center manager said he needed the most. But I really want to work on computers. I'm going to put 'I assembled my PC' on my resume when I build my own computer. But I'll take the TV repairman job if I get the offer."

"Scraps, kid. Scraps is all ya gonna make at the Asbesto Buy's service center. Might make you're first million after ya work there fifty years. I's gots a better idea how me an' you can make a fortune." The old man motioned with his index finger for the boy to come closer. "I've got one word for ya. Listen up." The old man whispered in John's ear. "Honeysuckles."

"What?"

"We gonna sell honeysuckles at the supermarket. Tomorrow you take that banana boat of yours an' ya fill it full with every single one of those great tasting flowers ya can get yo' hands on at that cove. I'll take care of all the business negotiations with the Schnucks supermanager. We'll be able to party a solid year with the profits I split with ya right down close 'nough the middle. 60-40."

The boy questioned Don's business venture, "I don't think that will work."

"Dammit. You drive a hard bargain. It's my idea, but I do half an' half with ya anyway 'cause I'm the charitable type. 50-50. What da ya say?"

John looked at the old man doubting he had 20-20 vision.

"Kid, I know what I'm talkin' 'bout. I know how to make money. I've made millions. I've made $58,243,292 to date in my life so the guy countin' my moneys tell me. My accountant a good one. Got four eyes to count with. Said I could write this here computer off as a business expense since I usin' it for my work. Workin' on writin' my livin' expenses here off, too, since I'm only usin' this place to write. That's 'bout all I'm gonna do here. Like anybody could call a two bedroom two bathroom shack a house! My Bahamas hacienda, smallest I got, is ten times as big as this apartment! My Long Island mansion next door to Billy Joel gots a garage five times as big as this. My penthouse in Las Angeles got a kitchen twice as big 'cause I always eat out in L.A. Even it's got a bigger fridge. And more booze, too." Don spoke in a secretive voice. "But I got the wet bar out of L.A. It's in storage with the jukebox."

"How many houses do you have?" John spoke trying to hide his disbelief.

"I know I gots at least ten last time I checked." Don whimpered, "'cause that's what my accountant says I'm payin' taxes on. Summer house in Wyoming, winter house in Puerto Rico, spring house in Hot Springs, Arkansas, the fall house in Vermont is my property. Mine. All mine. My property. Chateau in Versailles, France is mine, I tell ya. So is the coffee plantation in Belize, Central America."

"Why are you living here?"

"The bitches got it all!" Don cried with Ray Charles in the CD player. "I'm busted. The cows are all dry and the hens won't lay and I gots a big stack of bills gettin' bigger each day." Don reached into his pocket and upon finding the pocket was empty resorted to wiping his hand, filled with the contents dripping from his nose, onto his pants. "Each damn ho'." He blew. "The sluts took all my money!"

"How did you make so much?"

The CD player began playing Barry Manillow. The song changed Don's tune. He sung along, "I wrote the very best love story. I put the words and the scenes together. I am Don Juan. I write the stories makin' the whole world of wives happy to see the hubby when he gets home from work. I write the songs of love and steamy romance. I write the songs that make the housewives horny. I write the stories. I write the stories." Don wiped his hands for a minute. He carefully pulled one of the books stacked on the coffee table and held it in front of the boy.

John read aloud the cover title. "The Spy Who Shagged Me." The words, Don Juan Domingo, were on the front cover.

"I'm gonna let you hold this here book. You be careful with it. Don't get no snot on it or nothin'. Ok? Read the inside cover."

"Don Juan Domingo is Agent 0007"

The old man interrupted, "The extra Oh is for ya know what."

The boy continued, "of her Majesty's Secret Service sent on a secret mission to sabotage the evil Dr. Prude's plot to steal the Queen of England's crown jewels. Don Juan Domingo, poised as Buckingham Palace's groundskeeper overhears while tending the lawn not only are the Queen's prized petunias to be pruned but so is the Queen's favorite bedroom servant. The uncovering of a plot to murder the Queen in her bed is only the beginning. Agent 0007 saves the flowers to the satisfaction of the Queen, and Oh! is she satisfied. Don Juan Domingo like you've never read before!"

"This book sold over a fifty thousand copies. The scene makin' it so popular is when Domingo rolls around on a bear skin rug with a Russian spy. Ya know what I mean by rollin' 'round, don't ya?"

The boy nodded his head in affirmation.

"She, it was a lady spy, of course, tells him he has to vacuum the shag carpet or else she'll tell the Queen it was Domingo, not her, who cut the petunias. Housewives loved it and I got to take a magic carpet ride 'round the world from the moneys I made."

"But the cover says the flowers weren't cut."

"No it don't. It says the flowers saved to the Queen's satisfaction. Agent 0007 sticks 'em in a vase an' gives 'em to her in the mornin'. She was satisfied good an' plenty. Take a look at my picture in the back cover."

John saw a photograph resembling the old man except this picture was of a much younger individual.

"I was a handsome man twenty five years back. Not that I'm sayin' I ain't a heartthrob now. 'Cause I am. More sexy than ever. Almost made People magazine Sexy Man of the Year and I woulda if I had rub elbows with that chief lady editor like Sean Connery did."

"Wasn't there a movie with the same title?"

"All ya kids do is watch TV. My book better! When my lawyers get done with him that swindler gonna pay me royalties for stealing my book name. Lawyer tells me might get his house, too."

"You don't have any money left?"

Don's eyes shifted. His facial complexion became a shade darker in tone. He spoke in a concealed manner, "Listen to this here story but don't you tell nobody what you hear I say 'cause I claim it all hearsay. OK?"

"Ok."

"Back in '76 my fifth wife left me in Carson, Nevada 'cause she wanted to listen to Johnny Cash sing an' I didn't want to. So I had to hitchhike back to LA, my closest home, 'cause my fourth wife I divorced a week prior got a lawyer to cancel all my credit cards. Stinkin' lawyers. I'll do anything to get a lift so when I get picked up by this trucker I say I'm a famous writer. And sure 'nough she give me a ride 'cause she read every book I wrote. Now tellin' her I was a famous writer was a big mistake 'cause I could tell right away Bernice, that what she told me her name was, wanted to put the truck in park and play with the Tonka between my legs. I didn't 'unt her to grab my stick 'cause she was one big broad. Barely 'nough room in the seat for the two of us. Under normal circumstances that wouldn't bothered me much but my fifth wife had just picked my pockets clean an' I just wasn't up to a big gal feelin' 'round in my pants. Ya know the feelin' don't ya?"

John shook his head.

"Listen. Big Bertha was so big she didn't have to leave her seat to get a tire. She had a spare around her waist. Eighteen of 'em. She was almost as wide as a semi an' she coulda smothered me if she coulda rolled herself on top of me."

"I thought you said her name was Bernice."

"Bernice. Bertha. Who cares? Both big woman names. Anyway, she gets me talkin' 'bout my books and hows I got to be so famous. And she gets to sayin' how all her fellow female truckers loves me an' reads to each other over the CB my writin'. Next thing I know we in Las Vegas, not Las Angeles. She pulls up to the drive thru of something lookin' like a McDonalds 'cause it had arches that the truck drove underneath an' says something about gettin' hitched and needin' my autograph. I thinks she's gotta swap trailers an' I'm puttin' my signature on her legal lookin' form to swap trailers 'cause its gots the word, 'license', on top. Didn't look at it too close. Thought the M was for motor and the V for vehicle. Put my autograph on just 'bout anything 'cause I'm that kinda of guy for my fans. Never again! Big Bertha tricked me! Before I knew what had happened I was rollin' down the highway bound for Muskogee, Oklahoma where she from with wife number six. Wouldn't have got that far but she told me we is gonna party there an' I got a rule 'bout never passin' up a party. How was I suppose to know when we park the trailer in front of a trailer home in the trailer park, it's a weddin' party? That's when I found out I done got hitched all right. Ow! Started cryin' but they gave me some home brewed whiskey an' after I get to drinkin' some I get to thinkin' we can make this work since they make such great tastin' whiskey an' all. Just tie the trailer home to the semi-truck an' she can drive me 'round while I drink n' write. Don't even have to stop to pee 'cause the home came with a built in outhouse. Done some good writin' on the road. Done some of my best writin' with my drawers dropped to my feet. Gots the best of both worlds in this situation. So we cruisin' back to L.A. 'cause her folks and a hundred of her closest relatives, brothers, sisters, cousins, all the same thing in Oklahoma, wants to see where we gonna live. Now I tells them I don't have space in my penthouse for all 'em, which wasn't quite right but who in their right mind would put a hundred Okies from Muskogee a hundred floors in the air. They ground people. Get airsick for sure. I had a plan. Hef owe me a big favor, so what's I was going to do is drop all 'em off at Hef's mansion so the Okies could shack up there for awhile. They like the idea 'cause it turns out the Beverly Hillbillies their favorite TV show. Naturally, I would have to house the displaced inhabitants from the Playboy Mansion for a spell. Life is good. I'm happy an' enjoying the ride then ya know what happened?"

"No. What happened?" John was enthralled.

"Johnny Carson was playin' on the radio about eleven at night. I tells her to change the station 'cause I don't think Johnny funny but Bertha don't unt to 'cause she likes to stay up late and listen to him before she fall asleep at the wheel. I gets to havin' a discussion with her 'bout how bad drivin' an' sleepin' at the same time can be to yo' health. She says on the straight stretches in Kansas she fall asleep with her tummy 'gainst the wheel all the time. Sometimes she say she wake up just in time for breakfast findin' herself headin' straight for the truck stop diner. I tell her see what happens when 'yo stomach do the steerin'. I change the station 'an there some gal readin' parts of my book, From Here to There. I tells Bertha I deserve royalties from her readin' my stuff over the radio an' she gets to disputin' the matter with me 'cause she do it all the time. Next thing I know we both fighin' for the wheel. But I tell her I'm a gentleman an' the proper thing to do is for us to get divorced. She heart broken but she reluctantly agree so we drive down to Baja, Mexico where I get unhitched from her. Being the nice man I am I tell her I'd dedicate my next book to her an' I did. Called it L.A. Hitcher Hickuppin' to Las Vegas. So there ya have it."

"Have what?"

"Have that. Kid, can't you listen good?"

"What's this have to do with"

"Oh. Oh. Oh. My fault, kid. See what happens when ya get up in years. Ok." Don's lowered the volume of his voice again. "I'm in Baja. Walk into this cantina an' I get to dancin' with this senorita. She looks sort of sinister but my tamale tells me all she needs is a little of my hot love sauce to make her edible. An' sure 'nough when she got heated up an' gets some of my secret love condiment on her she turns out to be all right. Nice girl. Just lost. Facin' the wrong direction. Needed someone to turn her 'round an' I, being the helpful kinda of man I am, did just that. So after words, we get to talkin' and turns out she speaks perfect American which is a good thing 'cause the only Spanish words I know is 'La Bomba.' Turns out me and her had the same friend, Jose Cuervo, so we gots lots in common to talk 'bout. She says her name Alberta Capone and her daddy is none other than the same Chicago mobster with the identical last name. She spends the summers in Canada and the winters in Mexico livin' off papa's fortune the FBI never found. I showed up 'bout when she almost out of money. Should have left her when I found out she broke. That what my last wife did to me. Damn smart slut. Anyway, Alberta convince me we can be the next Bonnie an' Clyde. I willin' to give anything a try once 'cause I got a dash of adventuresome in me. She make a plan to rob a bank, the biggest one in downtown Tijuana 'cause she don't like the banker there, it being her ex an' all. I tell her I ain't gonna do no stick up. I'm no stinkin' dirty thief. She say all I have to do is get the Swiss bank account numbers out of the safe. That more like it. Don't have to get my white collar dirty or nothin'. Ya can never have 'nough money ya know. An extra twenty million might come in handy for a rainy day. I agree. She know the combination since her ex-husband was also an ex-con an' the prison tattoo he got on his butt the same as the combo to the safe. I took her word for it. Mark my words, kid. Never trust a dark skinned senortia named Capone livin' in Tijuana, Mexico. I sneak into the bank late Friday nite 'an I see this magazine called Banker's Digest on the hotshot ex convict banker's desk. The urge to let a load loose befalls me. Never drink the water in Mexico, kid. So I'm sittin' on the bank crapper readin' Banker's Digest. See this ad printed by the law firm of Ernesto Schwab & Suarez. The ad say we make money for our client the old fashion way. We embezzle it.

Even gets a free vacation to Belize when ya pay one grand, baby money to me, for one of their consultations. Write down the number to their Tijuana office an' that's when I hear Alberta's voice. She sayin' 'where he at Diego?' over and 'er. I'm 'bout to yell back 'I'm usin' the shitter.' But I remember my manners 'bout being polite to a lady 'cause I just got done readin' Ann Landers column on the proper way to stand in line at a bank. So I don't yell. Woulda not known to yell in a bank, otherwise. Good thing 'cause I hear her ex-husband's voice. Turns out I'm set up to be the fall guy for this ex con's next con. I was gonna get framed when they lock me in the vault an' they takes off with the last measly million left from her Uncle Al's fortune."

"I thought you said Al Capone was her father."

"Father. Uncle. All the same thing when you're part of the mob. I was just checkin' to make sure ya payin' attention, kid. Ya followin' me, Ok?"

"Ya."

"Good. 'Cause I forgot where I at."

John reasoned the old man was suffering from the same illness that led to Al Capone's demise. The old man had dementia. "You're in St. Louis, Missouri."

"What that got to do with my senorita story?"

"Sorry. You were in a bank with Alberta Capone and her ex-husband the banker who was also an ex-convict."

"That's right. When the two of 'em run into the bank vault lookin' for me ya know what I did?"

"No what?"

"I locked them in the vault. Told 'em I was gonna call Geraldo an' tell him I found Al Capone's secret stash. Whata ya lookin' at me like that for? Geraldo's Secret Slaying Service was advertising a special in the Digest. No hush money up front. Ya just buy the first five bags of cement. They do the rest. Quietly. Always wanted to bury someone alive behind a wall of cement. Here my chance to do two for one. The ad in the Digest had a coupon to do four feet for the price of two. I make the call. Alberta starts hummin' a new tune. She was comin' 'round.

Apparently she no longer desired the side of the vault she had boxed herself in this here love triangle she had created. Can't blame her. Angles all wrong. One too many guys an' one too few a gal. Better to be in a Grecian square with four legs capable of doin' greater than ninety degrees." Don demonstrated with his fingers. "An' ya didn't think I knew nothin' 'bout stretch her nometry. The Secret Service show up an' Alberta is bawling harder than Lucille as they chain her up. But the banker was tough. Nothin' new for him. I say to myself, 'Poe, I is not. I will not let Alberta squash my grapes of wrath. I'm a rich man 'cause I got a full bottle of wine on top of every Steinbeck piano in every house of mine. An' I gonna get richer when I give Swab a call 'cause I won't need a maid to mop my yacht's deck.' So I told the masons to let her go."

"What happened to the banker?"

"The hell with him! One less banker the better off the world I'm thinkin'. Well, Alberta gets to thankin' me for savin' her an' she starts huggin' on the masons, too, to show her gratitude. Banker slipped loose. Don't know how. Guess he use to wearin' concrete shoes. If ya can find him ya can find what's left of Capone's money. The search for him is another story I tell ya later. So there ya have it. The moral to the story is trust yo' lawyer, not yo' banker. 'Cause callin' Ernesto Schwab & Suarez is the best phone call I ever made."

"I don't understand."

"Of course not. I'm not done. Hold your horses, kid."

Don whispered. "I can't tell ya who the person was I talked to on the phone 'cause I never met 'em in person. Told me I was guaranteed confidentiality that way. They tell me to wire ten thousand U.S. dollars to the Cayman Islands 'an they buy me a $9000 house there for me. They keep ten percent. That fair. From then on they tell me to tell my ex-wives I'm takin' a yearly vacation to that house. I been doin' so every year since '76 right after my start of summer vacation right after my end of June vacation but before my July 4th vacation. Always do my July 4th vacation in the U.S. 'cause that's the kind of American I am. The

154

patriotic type. Never can get 'nough vacationin', ya know. I put on my taxes the house in the Caymans always in need of repairs an' that's why I leave the country with ten thousand dollars to fix it up, but I don't go direct to the Caymans. I stop in Belize, first, an' make a ten thousand dollar deposit at Bank de Suarez. Look just like a Swiss bank on the outside. Ten thousand goes in every year an' the same ten thousand come out a year later which I have dutifully used to add value to my Cayman Island mansion which used to be the size of this here apartment. Suarez tell me it ain't just one shack size no mo'. Couldn't tell ya. Never seen the place. I pay 'em ten grand a year to do all the upkeep. So I ask you a question to ponder young lad. How does this scheme make me money?"

John scratched his brow. He was interested in the old man's story. He wished he could have saved more. More than the thousand dollars he had slaved all year to save. The sum of the money produced from his saved money was twenty dollars.

"You've been collecting interest from your Belize bank account with ten thousand dollars for almost twenty five years. You must have fifty hundred thousand saved."

"That right! You a smart kid, but you off by a couple hundred thousand."

But why do you each year put ten thousand in and take ten thousand out?"

The old man lowered his voice. He was barely audible. "'Cause none of my ex-wives knows about my Belize bank account. No one knows. Even Suarez an' Schwab ain't gonna tell no one on account they both dead as doornails. May the good Lord rest my humble money makin' servants' souls."

"How did they die?"

"Guess I'm not the only one readin' Banker's Digest 'cause when I made my deposit withdrawal last year there was two big blocks of cement at the doorway an' the bank had a new name, Bank de Diego. Banks changin' names all the time, ya know."

"Don't you have to report the income earned from your Belize bank account to the IRS?"

155

"What! Wait a second. What you implyin'? Schwab & Suarez told me their money makin' scheme completely legit as long as none of my ex-wives don't find out." The old man shouted, "An' squeal to Uncle Sam!" The old man spoke with shame, "Kid, don't look at me like that. Big Brother Sam got 'nough money. Don't need my piece. That quarter a million barely 'nough for me to get by on now that I'm retired an' my pen quiet in my old age. It my IRA. They don't tax that. It all I got left. Awe, what the hell I tellin' ya all this for. Complete moot point 'cause I can't get the moolah tell next summer. I'm livin' off what's leftover after my ex-wife cashes in my royalty checks. Nothin'!"

"Did you marry Albeta Capone?"

Don tired his best to control any indication of anger in his voice, nevertheless, he was undoubtedly perturbed with the boy's question. "No, I did not. I'm not gonna get tied to the mob. Even my getting' hitched to trucker Bertha weren't legal since I signed the m license with my pen name, not my real name. Thank the Lord. Wish the God damn lawyer woulda told me that sooner. Take that last sentence back. Really shouldn't say bad things 'bout lawyers 'cause without 'em ya can't get divorced."

"Kid, let's change the subject. My turn to ask ya a question."

John nodded his head.

"Ya got any girlfriends?"

A few moments went by. The boy looked out the old man's patio window when he replied. "No."

"Well when the last time ya been on a date?"

John tried the best he could to cover any shakiness in his voice. His jaw trembled as he spoke, "I'm too busy with work." His head dropped. "I never meet anyone."

"What! There woman all over this this town. Population fifty fifty mix. Nothing near as bad as San Francisco. There two million people in St. Lewey. Give me a minute to do my 'rithmetic. Where a calculator when ya need one. Got it! You got a million women to choose from. That nothin' like the selection in a city like New York but it good 'nough."

"Most of those women are married or are older than me."

"Didn't think of that, kid. That the 'vantage of being an older man. Gots a wider selection of younger women to choose from. So how long ya lived in these here apartments?"

"Almost two years."

"How many girls ya meet here in that time?"

A minute went by before John responded, "One."

"I been here a month an' I 'ready met a hundred in this apartment complex alone," Don looked at the boy staring motionlessly at the patio window "but they younger for me. Tad too old for a twenty year old lad. Then 'gain, ya shouldn't knock an older woman 'til ya tried one out. Ya learn a lot."

John's eyes focused again on the apartment's interior.

"Kid, ya can help me out. Need ya ta do me a favor. Don't get 'round like a used to."

John's thoughts reentered the room. "What can I do for you?"

"I need ya to go downtown to the law offices of Thompson & Coburn 'an sign some papers. Got a lawyer there. Cost me a $20,000 retainer but I got the best whole lawyer in the wide Midwest to take care of my ex-wives problems. Not as good as a California one, but good 'nough. They gets more practice with divorce over there. Hell, in Hollywierd, divorce law is by law the only kind they permitted to practice. Should have shacked up there."

"How many times have you been married?"

Before the boy had finished speaking his last word the old man without warning erupted like a volcano, "Don't you say the M word while you're in my house ever 'gain! You'll not use that four letter fuckin' profane word in my presence. Ever! Got it!"

"But marry is a five letter word."

"No, it is not. M-E-R-R-Y is the five-letter word ya thinkin' of. That a good word 'cause it used in reference to partyin'. Don't they teach you kids how to spell in school nowadays?" Don didn't wait for the boy to respond. "An you'll only use the word W-I-F-E," Don spelled the word, "when ya say it in the

157

same sentence as cookin'. Or cleanin'. Ya gotta use that word in the right context or else it a bad word, too. Ya better wash yo' mouth out with soap tonight young man, or else ya gonna develop a vulgar mouth."

"So how many times have you been?" John waited cautiously, prepared to run for cover at the slightest indication of fumes venting from Don's temple.

The old man did not explode, instead, he cried for five minutes nonstop. His tears fell like rain. "Damn unluckiest number. I knew I should have stopped at twelve! That last bitch tricked me into slappin' a ring on her finger before she let me slap my love pinky in her stinky. I tell ya that's what it was! Smelled just like this apartment. Now I've got thirteen lawyers lookin' to skin me. That not quite right. Wife thirteen alone gots thirteen lawyers fishin' for my money."

"You've been married thirteen times?"

"Pretty sure. If ya want the exact count ya have to talk to my lawyer. What are ya lookin' at me like that for? I tell ya not a one of 'em was my fault! Let me show ya what did in my last carriage. Yes, I said carriage. Don't look at me like that. I'm not senile. That as close as I'm gettin' to sayin' that nasty word rhymin' with carriage."

Don dug through the papers on his naked lady desk for ten minutes. John patiently waited. The old man held a paper in both hands for a minute. A tear from his eye fell on the paper.

"Her name was Cindy. With flowing locks of golden braids an' a smile so sweet she made an aging man feel like a lad in a candy store. Every time I rode atop her carriage I was once again a steed in full prime. I called her my Cinderella. I loved her so. Why am I talkin' like that? I don't like her no mo'. She tricked me! She told me the pumpkins she had on that quarter of a century year old chassis of hers was all natural home grown. Then she said they were gonna stay planted underneath her dress 'til I carry her. So I said to myself I'm gonna do things right this time. It taken me twelve times but I finally learned my lessons. Gonna wait this time. Do things the right way. An' it was two days later after our weekend whirlwind courtship I finally got to take a peak at her unearthed pumpkins in our Niagara Falls honeymoon suite. Floatin' in the Jacuzzi! Her balloons man made! Artificial! But I can deal with that 'cause we equal since she gotta cope with watchin' me take off my head of hair an' put it on the dresser every night. So a month go by an' I'm happy 'cept for when I come home every day from a hard day of work an' notice she's gone shoppin'. Grocery shoppin'! She eatin' a whole pumpkin pie by herself every day. A year later she'd gotten so big when she went regular woman shoppin' she came back emptied handed. She said they couldn't fit her dress size number on any of the labels of any of the dresses that fit her. Well times gettin' tough 'cause the royalty checks ain't getting' mailed to my door every day like they used to, but I'm not gonna let my wife run 'round barefoot an' naked outside. Gets some good advice from the guy workin' at the tire company where I had to go 'cause I needed bigger wheels put on my new car 'cause the tires a 'vette come with not sporty 'nough. He says his wife got the same problem an' so he called his boss at the tire company to have her dress custom made. I do the same. When it came back even it don't have no dress size on the tag. Just letters. B-L-I-M-P. After that, I didn't feel like eatin' no mo' of her cherry pie. Not that it mattered 'cause I couldn't find it if I wanted to! She never did any cookin'! She was a bad wife. Read this poem I wrote for her on our one-year edding anniversary. If ya can't read it all 'cause of the pumpkin pie stains lets me know an' I'll read it for ya."

John read aloud,

"Woman. You can't live with 'em. That's why you write poetry.

Beyond your dress, do your tresses inch as far as I can see,
With hair colors more radiant than an evening sky.

One day like no other day though a year older you may
be,
Without a doubt I heard you pout another year gone by.

Never forget to admit "Life is a party" is the key,
These simple four words of wisdom to drink can be no
lie."

Don helped with the last line. "What da ya think? 'Cause I'm
thinkin' this poem is a work of art rightfully belongin' in the
Smithsonian. Spent a whole ten minutes writin' the prose on a
fancy paper napkin at the fine eatery I took a friend of mine on
the night prior me givin' it to my ife. When she, it was a lady
friend, who I took out for her birthday, went to make a call I said
to myself, 'I'm not doin' anything else. Might as well patch up
things with my ife.' So I remember to give it to her on time,
never did that for no ife 'fore mostly on 'count I never been
arried a 'hole year 'fore, an' she use it to put a piece of pie on.
I'm thinkin', 'What's the matter with her? Can't she use a plate?'
But I don't say nothin'. Then she starts cryin' an' says I'm
makin' fun of her gettin' porky. There nothin' in that prose 'bout
her blowin' up to blimp size like she had. Then she say it a
stupid poem 'cause it don't even rhyme right. Then she says I'm
not what I was. I say, 'I a has been? At least I use English
proper.' She say I don't know how to hold my pen no' more. I
say, 'How ya know? Ya spend all yo' time locked in the
bathroom lookin' at that magazine with Sean Connery on the
cover.' Then she say, 'Your'e a lousy wrinkled washed up
writer.' I yell, 'How dare ya call me wrinkly. I not nearly as
wrinkly as Sean, but you likes him mo'. Wrinkly a divorcin'
word.' She say, 'That's right. I'll sign first,' an' tries grabbin'
my writin' pen from me. We get to fightin'. She get the pen. I
struggle with her for it 'an that's when catastrophe struck the
Hindenburg. I popped one her balloons! Now she leakin', nearly
deflated, an' lookin' lopsided. Her lawyer say it gonna take
every penny I got to pay the doctor to fill her back up with e

steam. Is that what they put in those things now days 'cause I thought they just switched to saline? Still don't know what the letter e got to do with it. She say no one wanna carry her no mo'. I say it 'cause no one strong 'nough to. Can ya believe how things turn out? Only night 'fore I'm thinkin' she gonna happily scribble with my favorite pen all night long an' look what happened. This year has turned out to be a anything but a good year." Don dug his face in his hands.

Until BB King started playing on the CD player. He sung along,

> "I gave you a brand new Ford
> You said, 'I want a Cadillac.'
>
> I bought you a $10 dinner
> You said, 'Thanks for the snack.'
>
> I let ya live in my penthouse,
> You said, 'It was just a shack.'
>
> I gave ya seven children,
> An' now ya wanna give 'em back."

John thought to himself. He no longer doubted the old man was a writer, and apparently had made a great deal of money. But surely the man had not made $58 million in his life. Nor did John believe the Don had been married thirteen times. The old man had said he was seeing a doctor. Did Don Murphy have Alzheimer's Disease? No matter what illness had befallen the old man, John took pity on him.

"Do your kids" John stopped. He couldn't think of how to finish the sentence.

"Ain't got no kids, kid. Got thirty-two step kids, but not of one of 'em is really mine. Pretty sure it's thirty-two. Lawyer knows for sure."

"Your step kids know" John paused mid sentence again.

"What? Half of 'em wouldn't even know my name unless ya told 'em I'd been married to one of their step moms. They might not even recognize me then. Wait a second." Don's eyes sparkled. "My tenth wife inherited from her third husband a step son same age as her. Two of them used to hang out together all the time. Can't remember his name but he a real cool cat. He could party good." Don picked up his telephone. "Think he livin' in Memphis now. He might want to party." He put the handset back down. "Maybe that not so good an idea since she livin' in Memphis too an' since she his." Don stopped. "How 'bout me an' you go to Memphis an' party with BB King on Beale Street tomorrow?"

"I've got to work tomorrow. I don't have the money to go to Memphis."

"I forgot I broke too, kid. Ya a good kid. Ya can sign those lawyer papers for me can't ya?"

"Ya. Do you want me to drive you to the law office?"

"No, kid. Lawyer don't need me there. Already made my hand numb signin' my autograph in the office last week. Lawyer just need yo' John Hancock. Just legal third party stuff. She said anyone can sign even someone off the street can sign. But I'd be much obliged if you do the honors."

"When do you want me to do it?"

"Soonest next appointment I could get is in two weeks. Busy lawyer. Got lots of divorcin' to do. Give ya a freebie. Normally, I wouldn't do this for no one but you cool. Tell this line to the lawyer. Gotta a good feelin' it'll work for ya. Would try it myself but I'm retired. You just say ' I don't have time for a lot of fun.'"

"Why?"

"Kid, ya haven't even kissed a girl have ya?"

The old man had told John a lot about himself. His emotional distraught over his last failed marriage was clearly evident to John. John had never felt, in his twenty three years of existence, such emotion. He had never kissed a girl, and until now he was ashamed of this fact. But how could he feel ashamed

162

in the presence of this old man who clearly was in much worse condition than himself?

"No."

"Well don't ya worry none. This lawyer get your groove thing back. You be on your feet in two weeks. I knows so. Once ya get ya balls rollin' again ya be back on the right track. I feel bad for ya not havin' scored an' me braggin' so much. Haven't felt this sorry for nothing 'cept myself when I lost my last good bottle of Glen Livet. But ya saved it for me. You take my apology. I know ya will 'cause you a good person."

Don gave the boy the same look of concern as when John pulled his bottles out of the trashcan. This time the old man's concern was sincere. He put his hand on John's shoulder. Don rubbed his shoulder blade gently. John felt like the man was trying to infer something by this action. The boy was very uncomfortable with the touch.

The old man looked at the boy like a doctor does a patient, "Ya stroking it aren't ya?"

"I don't."

"You're not yankin' yo' yonker?" Don examined the boy's facial expression. "Not slappin' yo' salami?" He looked at the boy again. "You not even masterin' baitin' when ya all alone at the lake?"

"I don't feel like it."

"Got just what you need." Don picked up one of the magazines on the table. "Take this mag. Some entertainment for men. 'Course ya gotta play with yourself. Look at Miss July once in the morning and once in the evening. If ya get the urge to touch yourself ya go righta head. Just don't tell me 'bout it. Don't wanna know. An' if ya get the pages stuck together ya go 'head and keep it. I got three more copies just like her in my closet."

"I can't."

"Son, ya gotta get that stuff out of ya. It's toxic. You've seen what happens when a girl gets a load of that stuff in her, haven't ya? Her belly swell up something awful. Don't worry about

163

goin' blind. Ya look at ya palms every day. If ya see some new hair sproutin' ya stop strokin'. Don't worry 'bout the hair 'cause it'll fall off when ya stop. An' ya palms get hairy long before ya lose your sight."

Don handed the July '76 Playboy magazine to John. "I've done it. Only thing I did for two weeks solid back in '86. Look at me. I can see good 'nough. An' I got more hair on my head than I got on my hands." He waved his hands in front of John in a back and forth manner.

John took the magazine in hand.

"Ya go home an' practice the line I gave ya. 'Don't have time for a lot of fun.' Go 'head an' take my computer, too. They said the thing can do cut and copy word processin' an' it didn't even come with some scissors."

John was not nearly as hesitant about the offer to borrow the old man's computer but he tried, "Are you sure?"

"I don't have enough space. Barely 'nough room in this shack for all the paper I gonna write on. Might have to paste some on the wall 'cause I'm already outta space of the flo'."

John picked up the computer, monitor, keyboard, and mouse in one swoop. He dropped the magazine. The old man set the monthly on top of the pile of computer equipment John carried.

Don waived his hand to the boy in a back and forth manner as he closed the patio door for John. John assumed Don was trying to wave good-bye as best an arthritic old man could.

Don thought to himself, "Oh my God! I've never been in so bad shape before where I didn't even wanna play with myself. He's really sick."

The boy's walk back to his apartment was carefree. For the first time in months he felt a warm feeling inside his self for John knew he had made a friend. Being a supermarket stocker, he was accustomed to carrying an assortment of items at once like the ones Don Murphy had given him. Still, he took great care with the parts, as if he were holding a newborn baby, when he opened the door to his apartment building. He didn't see the girl next door, the one he had spoken to briefly on Saturday, while she was checking her mail.

Doris could not see her new neighbor's face but she could see his arms and legs flexing. A new neighbor with tone muscles! Then she saw her neighbor's face when he closed the apartment building door. John wasn't looking at her. He looked so unhappy. After looking at him, she felt bad about telling Don her neighbor was a loser. She was going to call Don tonight but she was reluctant as she was filled with shame. Until the Playboy magazine fell to the ground. She was going to call Don immediately and tell him she was absolutely right about her neighbor. Not only was the computer nerd a loser, he was a pervert, too. He was a very, very sick person.

CHAPTER 20

Go walk your dog, Ward.

His son wasn't home. Mr. O'Reilly peeked into his daughter's room. Kathy was counting her Barbie dolls. He listened.

She pointed at the first doll. "One."

She pointed at the second doll. "One zero."

She pointed at the third doll. "One one."

She pointed at the fourth doll. "One zero zero."

His four year old daughter was counting her Barbies in binary. Correctly. She had over a hundred dolls. Good. John's daughter was going to be preoccupied for two minutes. Mrs. O'Reilly wasn't in his daughter's room. Very good. Where was she? Because Mr. O'Reilly wanted to count in binary his wife's body parts. Two on her front side in particular. Over and over again.

He glimpsed in their adjacent bedroom. She wasn't there. Too bad. She wasn't in the hallway bathroom. Not in the living room nor in the dining room. She certainly wasn't in the study. He had just come from there but he double checked to make sure. Was he going to study her in the study? He would like to do a report on her lower back. Verbally. Whispering softly the results to her in her ear. Maybe doing a taste test of her ear lobes would be a more effective reporting technique. There was no subject to study in the den except biology. From a textbook. No good. He wanted more than words. He wanted to play with his real life playmate. She wasn't downstairs. If she was she was walking in the dark. All the lights downstairs were off. He turned them on. He would very much like to see her reveal her inner beauty to him. He wanted to watch her remove her clothes, showing her bare shell before his peeping eyes, right now. He tip-toed up the stairs to the wall opposite the kitchen. From his dining room vantage point he could see the kitchen table had

166

been cleaned. He could feel the vibration of heels on the floor. He poked his head around the corner.

He found her inspecting the contents of the refrigerator. Her back was turned to him. Excellent. He continued to inspect her body with his eyes. The red blazer she wore this morning had been replaced with a white t shirt. He could see her bra beneath the shirt. Outstanding. He knew how to undo this one with one hand. She stood on her toes briefly to look in the icebox. He didn't care what she was looking for. She wasn't going to find anything. He didn't take her eyes off her legs. Her calf muscles flexed. John flexed his legs to get a step closer, and to readjust his pants. She bent over to look down on the last shelf. No milk in the fridge but. He didn't move but his drawers did. Upward. His eyes had climbed to her derriere. His wife's skirt concealed her hips. Not the silhouette of her hips. Her curvature was clearly visible from his view standing behind her. The outline of something underneath his pants was clearly visible as well. She opened the fruit and vegetable container below the bottommost shelf. Empty. But she wasn't. As he looked at her bosom, the cups of her bra filled to support her hanging breast. Mrs. O'Reilly husband wanted to do some shopping with his wife. Grocery shopping. In the produce department. For melons.

He did not reach with his hand. Yet. He took his knee and softly rubbed the back of her leg with his kneecap. He wanted her as his nightcap. Not yet. He put his hand on his wife's back along the crease of her skirt. She was not startled. He put one finger on her skirt's zipper. He did not pull. Instead, he traced her spine with his other hand. With only one finger. He nudged gently with both fingers. She stood upright. Her spine was as erect as his love finger. He caught her hands, lifting them overhead. He spun her, releasing her hands upon his shoulders. He held her at her hips.

Mr. O'Reilly smiled. "Did I ever tell you how great you look in heels?"

Mrs. O'Reilly smiled back. "Not in the kitchen like this. Not lately."

"I'd like to."

"I know you'd like to. I could hear you prancing all over the house from here, Mr. Dashing. So I thought I'd put my heels back on so you could think about me doing some dancin' tonight."

John smiled.

"Don't know why you're in the kitchen."

Her husband's eyes pointed towards the bedroom.

She smirked back, "because you're not getting any dessert from me. Sugarplum." She smiled as her husband frowned. "You've been a bad boy. A very,very bad boy." She pinched him on the cheek like a grandmother. "You're not getting any. I'm tired. I've had a hectic day." And she pecked a kiss on her husband's cheek, like she would her son. Then she gave him a pat on the butt like a coach does for a pitcher who just gave up the winning run in the bottom on the ninth. "Nice try, John. You need to take a shower. A cold one. You stink. I could smell you from around the corner."

John limped back to his study. He could have used some assistance carrying his love cane. His wife certainly didn't want to help. He thought. "What was I thinking?" He looked at Pluto when he sat down in his study chair. "She broke you're love bat, too, didn't she boy?"

The dog, given as a gift to John from Don Murphy, looked up briefly at his current owner. His long slender black ears draped to the ground. Pluto put his head back on the blanket in the corner of the room next to the couch. At seventeen years of age, time was catching up with the old dog curled in a tight ball. His coat, originally a golden tan, had turned to a lackluster brown. He didn't sniff with his coal black nose like he used to. Most of the time his nose was dry. He didn't follow any of the O'Reilly family about the house like he used to. When Pluto was an adolescent his pure black tail used to wag nonstop. His son, when he was a terrible two-year old lad, had tried to tape a hand fan to the dog's tail. Junior was trying to help Dad figure out a way to fix a broken down air conditioner. The dog's tail still wagged occasionally when his master entered his presence. John looked at the dog. Pluto hadn't wagged his tail for him this evening.

The old dog had settled into a routine. As long as nothing interfered with the dog's modus operandi, Pluto was all business. Up in the morning at six to take care of business outside. Wake up master if master is not up at six to get him going so master could go about his business. Sometimes wait in the hallway next to the small room containing the dreaded water torture chamber for master. Why master does business there and not outside is unknown. Put mushy bone with plastic covering at master's feet. Why master trades mushy bone for food is unknown. Watch master remove mushy bone from plastic and spread it open. Watch master stare at inside of spread open mushy bone. Look at dry dog food put in bowl. Wait for Purina canned food because Purina is a better business since the canned food Purina makes taste better. Eat food in order to do more business later. Spit out heartworm pill put in Purina canned food. No room for heart shaped objects in business. Show the master teeth as master pries open mouth with bad morning breath to reinsert pill. Lick master's hand for food. Always looking for more business. Watch master wash hands since mouth smells the same as the poop outside. Sleep. All day. Call it the In Between Business Power Nap. Repeat twelve hours later with one significant difference.

The highlight of my dog life is the evening hunting expedition with my master. Actually, any one of the master's clan will do. If the little one forgets to close the door I can take care of business myself. When I hear the box in the hallway chime many times and the Sun is setting, bark at the top of my lungs to remind master and his clan of this very important event. Find the chain to drag master outside if necessary.

Today, Pluto wasn't barking. The dog needed some assistance getting his bark box wound up. There was a magic word, which when spoken, made the old dog feel like a pup again.

Mrs. O'Reilly entered the dog and his hunting companion's den with a leash in her hands. Boncoeur's 3-D computer generated image visor covered her husband's eyes. She attached each end to the proper recipient. Pluto wagged his tail with vigor as she fitted the dog with a doggie coat labeled Pluto or Bust. She lifted her husband's goggles.

He looked at the leash. "I don't think he's up to it."

"You need to."

"I'm busy."

"Walk. Your anus!"

On the word, walk, the dog jumped up from his resting position dragging the payload attached to the other end of the leash into the air with enough force to orbit Pluto. Maybe even the eighth planet circling the Sun. Mrs. O'Reilly kindly opened the front door for their evening excursion.

She waved good-bye "Have a nice walk, George Jetson."

By the time Mrs. O'Reilly had completed her sentence, the master and the follower were on the driveway, the launch pad for the expedition. Getting the follower off his rocker required only preliminary rockets. Full throttle on the thrusters was initiated at the mailbox upon jettisoning a sample of spent liquid dog fuel. The dog had no need to refuel at the trashcan that had somehow drifted through space and time to the garage. This evening's prior mission had turned into a complete disaster, requiring a complete scrubbing by the master's master before returning to home base, the blanket, was authorized.

With only barren concrete space between the mailbox and Sirius, the next door neighbor's dog on the far side of the Great Wooden Barrier, an all out burn requiring no intake of oxygen was necessary. The payload connected to a maximally taut chain dragged behind. Sirius was nowhere to be found beyond the Great Wooden Barrier. The Great Wooden Barrier was at the edge of Sirius's territory and who rightfully owned the boundary was of continual dispute. Pluto deployed his primary nighttime sensory equipment. His nose dug into the ground next to the neighbor's backyard fence. Pluto raised his left rear extremity to properly position his liquid ejection probe. The fence no longer belonged to Sirius.

A coal black dirt filled nose stored several samples requiring immediate processing by the Interneighborhood Rover's Secondary Nolightneeded Sensory Device. This device, Pluto's tongue, rapidly covered and uncovered his beak producing a red glowing beacon in the darkness. Sampling continued while a comet pair, rare in this part of the neighborhood, passed by followed by two emitting red beacons. Upon Astronaut O'Reilly providing clearance via the reign signal, Rudolf dragged his sleigh master over No Dog's Land giving chase to the automobile's taillights.

Pluto's mission was to search and sniff the ring of dog made asteroids around the Andromeda and rosemary shrubs in the front yard of a vacant house in one of the nearest adjacent neighborhoods to the O'Reilly residence on Clark Manor Circle. This voyage required Pluto's passenger to pull his own weight. Pluto could barely make the mile long trek pulling his own weight across the dormant grass in a mild St. Louis December. If his master wanted a free ride, O'Reilly was going to have find a team of Alaskan huskies to help, rent a harness at London's Klondike & Ski Rental, and figure out how to boot the team without a whip. Pluto didn't do business with anyone practicing negative reinforcement.

The pair made the journey to the shrubs, jogging the journey side by side. In the glow of the streetlights above Pluto's coat was golden hued. O'Reilly had checked his companion's tail along the way. Pluto's tail was a key indicator of how much fuel Pluto had remaining. At the start of each walk, Pluto pointed his gas gauge straight up in the air stiffer than a beagle. At the end of their nightly trip after all data in the form of spent liquid dog fuel had been transmitted, his tail dangled limp like a useless antenna. So did his tongue. Pluto completed his mission by adding another asteroid around the Andromeda shrub.

Pluto's tail was a little below horizontal with his spine. The ongoing mission to the Pleilaide's residence, the home of the man who had produced a household of seven sisters, the most in this galaxy of neighborhoods, would have to be postponed much to Pluto's chagrin. With seven teenage daughters, Mr. Pleilade talked as if he had the whole world upon his shoulders. O'Reilly always felt pity when he would converse with the man. And embarrassment. About the start of each lunar cycle, if any one of the seven were to greet Pluto, O'Reilly had to use every muscle in his body to withhold the dog's over enthusiastic desire to stick his sniffer under his greeter's dress. Mr. O'Reilly claimed he was only hitchhiker. He barely knew the dog attached to his leash.

No matter what the distance, on the return trip the two companions switched roles with the dog following O'Reilly like a tired horse being led to water. Tonight, Pluto opted to go into mule mode at the Farmer residence, the house across the street from the O'Reilly's home. His owner could finish the last fifty feet to his own territory by himself. Pluto was positive his fellow hunter knew the way home from here. He was going to take a breather next to a bush underneath the Farmer's Oak tree for a spell. Maybe sniff the air for any passing by spent liquid dog fuel particles aromatically stemming from the plant.

Sometimes O'Reilly carried the dog home. Pluto acted like a stubborn child, kicking his feet all the way but he would never bite. Pluto wasn't going to end his strike any time soon; however, O'Reilly wasn't in the mood to lift sixty pounds of squirming dried out doggy weight. He couldn't. O'Reilly's bladder was full of spent human liquid fuel. He looked. No cars. He yanked out his probe to do his business on the tree. Pluto wagged his tail to cheer him on. About time the master got with the program.

If this were any other Oak tree in any other neighbor's yard he would have contained his self. This tree belonged however, to a neighbor he wasn't particularly found of even though the Farmer's only child, Katy, was his little girl's best friend. Not that Kathy had a choice of childhood playmates close to her home to choose from. Of the fifteen houses on Clarke Manor Circle, the house with a transplanted Oak tree in the back yard was the only house sheltering a four-year old or any child under the age of ten.

Mrs. Christina Farmer's only preoccupation was maintaining their family home. Full time. Mrs. Farmer didn't have any other occupation and she didn't do any household cleaning. This was the full time maid's job. The Farmer's maid must have stipulated in his contract he doesn't do trash. For the past several weeks the trash can was left in the driveway apparently forgotten. One time for a week. The trash collector put the garbage can next to the house the following week. John helped his neighbor last week by placing the trashcan next to the Farmer's three-car garage.

Christina didn't have time to drag the trashcan into the garage. She did take the time to lavishly decorate the house. Mrs. Farmer had a Washington University B.A. in Architecture so she was qualified, overly so, for the job. She was nearly done with her Master's from Wash U., too. John didn't know what degree she was seeking. From the looks of the interior of their home, recently featured in Better Homes & Gardens, her degree had to pertain to interior design. Her B.S. might as well have been a M.R.S. degree. That's the job she obtained with her B.A.

Her husband, Mr. Robert Farmer was the Regional Vice President of Union Planter's Bank. During a passing conversation last year with his new next door neighbor, O'Reilly was informed by Robert, that he, at 28 years of age, was the youngest VP in the Union. He earned his B.S. in History from Columbia. He came from a family rich in a tradition of hard work. For seven generations the Farmers plowed the fertile ground of southeast Missouri. During the Great Depression his great grandfather not only endured, he prospered by shrewdly purchasing other farmer's land for pennies on the dollar. From a single bank in 1926, Farmer's Bank had grown to fifty branches in 1979. Tough times hit in 1987 when his father, Robert III, newly appointed as Farmer's President, was forced to fight, tooth and nail, a hostile takeover by MidAmerica Bank. From then on, Farmer's prosperity dwindled. To save Farmer's Bank from financial ruin his father entered into a merger with Union Planters in 2012. The name, Farmer's Bank, no longer existed.

Robert told his story of being very discouraged with not becoming the next president of Farmer's Bank. Robert IV's father did not hand over the presidency upon Robert's graduation from college. He had to work as a teller. Still, he told O'Reilly he learned more in four months doing menial labor in a bank compared to his four years at Columbia. O'Reilly found out Christina wasn't his first wife. Apparently his first wife, which Robert married the June after he graduated from Columbia, wasn't satisfied with his social standing in society as a teller. The relationship didn't amount to much John was told. They had no children. Robert IV was introduced to Christina at a party five years ago by Robert III. Robert and Christina married four years ago. Katy was the product of their union. Coincidentally, Christina's father was the President of Union Planters Bank.

In a passing conversation, Mrs. Farmer informed Mrs. O'Reilly she was having an Oak transplanted to the Farmer's yard. As a child, Christina had an Oak in her back yard to swing on. She wanted her daughter to have the same experience. The Oak's bark, flaking at the slightest touch, didn't appear healthy. This tree needed every drop of nitrogen humanly possible to survive the move to foreign soil in the dead of winter. O'Reilly zipped his pants back up.

Pluto sniffed the presence of another nocturnal hunter. O'Reilly observed Mr. Farmer in the front yard sticking a sign into the ground next to the curb. John tuned his thoughts on the Farmers from the negative to the positive. Christina took care of his little girl after preschool. Mrs. O'Reilly in turn took care of the Farmer's pet Terrier, Boxer, and the O'Reilly's took care of Katy when Mr. and Mrs. Farmer took an extended weekend vacation. About once a month if not more. Except lately.

Mr. Farmer didn't touch the trashcan. Did Boncoeur offer a trash service? Mr. O'Reilly was going to recommend if the Farmer's didn't have time to take of trash, maybe Boncoeur did. He walked to the front yard. Pluto joined him. His master wasn't heading for home base. He walked like he was on a new mission, of the search and destroy a trashcan type.

"You old dog, you." Mr. Farmer yelled at the old dog and his leader ten feet away.

John thought. "Did he see me at the tree? He prepared himself to say, "Sorry. Old dog had to go. Hope you don't mind. Pluto has a mind of his own."

John spoke. "Hi Rober..t." He added the 't' just in the nick of time. Mr. Farmer didn't like to be called Rob. He didn't like the way Mr. O'Reilly said his full name, either.

"Katy told me."

"What?"

"When your wife picked up your girl this afternoon she was hot. Katy said to me, 'what did Kathy's Mom mean when she said, 'your Daddy has made a new friend on the airplane. Would you like to come with me to the airport and meet her? You became a member of the mile high club didn't you?'"

O'Reilly thought, "Why did I have to choose to be the helpful with the trash kind of neighbor?" He wanted to change the subject. How about sharing some tales about the two neighbor's dogs?

O'Reilly enjoyed the story of Mr. Farmer buying a pure breed from the pet store. A mutt such as Pluto was not good enough for the Farmer's daughter. Mr. Farmer intended to breed the dog for financial gain as well, until the dog demonstrated his affection on Mrs. Farmer's leg. And then Mr. Farmer's leg. The next day Mrs. Farmer drove Boxer to his wife's veterinary clinic. Boxer has been singing soprano ever since and walking by human legs without even batting an eye after the castration operation. At least Pluto could pretend to be a tenor even though his wife had pickled him, too. Mr. Farmer didn't care for this tale. Might as well not add fuel to the fire.

"My wife caught me flirting with the stewardess."

"Don't tell me she's got a private dick tailing you."

"She doesn't need one. She's got the ears of a bunny." He grinned at Rob. " And hearing better than a jack rabbit."

175

O'Reilly read the sign Farmer had planted. "What are you putting the for sale sign up for?"

"Puttin' the house up for sale." Rob's voice was full of attitude, implying O'Reilly couldn't read. "You're going to be the only house on the block without Christmas lights this year."

O'Reilly threw the remark back in his neighbor's face. "That's right. You didn't put up any lights last year, either."

He knew where this conversation was heading. When Rob asked him what he did for a living when they met last year, he told him he was a computer consultant, even had a couple Fortune 500 companies as clients. That's when he found out Rob's salary was $400k and his wife didn't have to work like John's wife and Rob was up for a raise next year. And a promotion. The Farmers must have had the Jones as a previous next door neighbor.

"How was Thanksgiving? Your sister show this year?"

John closed his eyes. Rob had to know about his family background. Why his wife had to tell Christine he did not know. Rob had to know John didn't have a sister. He reopened his eyes.

"Just me and the wife and the kids. Stayed home in St. Louis again. How was yours?"

"Just got back from the Caribbean. Spent a week on the boat with the parents and the grandparents."

"Glad to hear it. Looks like Pluto's had enough for this evening. Take care, Rob." O'Reilly turned to walk home.

"Hey John. Might as well tell you."

O'Reilly turned around.

"You'll find out sooner or later. Better me than from the grapevine. Me and Christine are separatin'. Just don't get women nowdays. Thought this time would be different. After the baby she never got her figure back. Can't talk to her. She spends more time talking to the maid than she does with me."

O'Reilly listened. He nodded his head.

"Tell me Reilly. You been married twenty years. How you do it?"

His neighbor thought. John wanted to provide a good answer. Something to help his neighbor. The book he was reading prior to his walk had a good line. He was ready to speak, "Two trees planted in one garden grow together towards the same sunlight. Their branches becoming more intertwined through the years." To this line he would append his phrase "You're job when you grow at different rates is to help your life mate catch up and vice versa." Then he remembered the words the author attached to the line before and after John had read it the first time seventeen years ago.

"Read this manure I wrote, kid." John looked at his neighbor in a daze. Rob waited with impatience. "That symbolic to say they got the same shit to talk about."

John spoke, "My wife has got me trained like a dog. She can't cook dinner worth a damn. I've been eating the same cereal every night for years. But when you eat the same thing every night, sleeping with the same woman comes easy as eating a piece of pie. Never know what the new day will bring but I can tell you what I'll be doing in the eve. Eating a piece of the wife's dessert. She's the tart type but her plum pie has enough sugar in it for an old man like me." John walked towards his home. He turned around five steps later. "Good luck to you, Rob."

O'Reilly walked away with a smug smile on his face. If his wife heard a remark from anyone regarding her husband's opinion of her dinner cooking skills, a remark from Katy or Christina tomorrow regarding her dessert making skills would make amends.

At the moment the dog could care less about food. Pluto crawled into the O'Reilly home, his tail appearing to be attached to a greyhound finishing last place in the last race around the track of his career. Time for his nighttime nap, dreams of asteroid adventures and skirt sniffing, and the anticipation of tomorrow morning's business, non dry Purina dog food. Canned, of course. The dog had twenty-four hours to recuperate for his next race around the neighborhood dog track.

The tired dog curled up on the blanket beside his worn out master sitting on the couch beside him. John's head nodded as he sat. He was nearly asleep sitting on the couch when someone tapped on his shoulder.

"John, if you fall asleep now you won't make it to bed."

He opened his eyes, " I found out what Kathy was so upset about at the dinner table this evening. Talked to Rob in his front yard. He say's him and Christine are separating."

"That's not what she said. They're getting a divorce for sure. When I picked Kathy up this afternoon I told Christine about the little ego trip you took today." She watched her husband's back stiffen, "Out of nowhere she blurts out in front of the kids, 'I'm getting a divorce, too! I caught him with the secretary!' Then she asks me if I want to look at the compromising pictures taken by the private investigator she hired. In front of the kids no less. Then she wanted to know if I wanted to go shopping with her. I thought about it for a second and was about to say yes when she says, 'The boutiques in Naples, Florida are really nice. We'll have a great weekend getaway vacation together.'"

"That figures. Rob's putting the house up for sale."

"She's already put the house up for sale on the Internet. She's says it's already sold and she's already signed all the papers for her lawyer. Done deal."

John thought, "Is she taking the tree with her?" He didn't speak. He'd had enough talk about the Farmers. He smiled at his wife, "So you think I had a ego trip today?"

"No. I know you've had a tough day. Your friend, Ed Rolands, called. He told me about you're meeting. He wants you to call him tonight when you have time. Ed told me you told him you had to leave because you couldn't wait to come home to have a piece of my pot roast." She smiled with a sweet little wink from her right eye, "Tell him thanks for the complement." She kissed her husband on the cheek like a wife who had finished reading one of the books on the top shelf of the study bookcase. "I'll leave the door open for you when you want to come to bed, Ok?"

After the "Thanks for putting me on the wife's good side," John's conversation with Ed Rolands was all business. Ed wanted him to do another presentation in Florida tomorrow.

"No, I can't. It's not the money, Ed. It's the time. I'm really busy right now. I could make some time for IBM tomorrow. Maybe lunch." He put an apology on his face for the telephone. He spoke very kindly. "In St. Louis."

Ed called back fifteen minutes later. Done Deal.

"Expect five people for lunch including my boss, the big chief project manager whose head points in the direction of a decision."

"What can you tell be about the big chief? C'mon, Ed. Me and you go way back."

"This guy takes five white shirts to the cleaners every Saturday at precisely 8:00 am when the cleaner opens the doors. If the cleaner doesn't open the door at 8:01am, the big chief takes his shirts and the teepee to the cleaners down the street. I guess that's how this project manager got the nickname, the 'cleaner.' Career IBM since day one out of college 29 years ago. Total neat freak. Had to share a hotel room with him last week. He even makes sure his toothbrush points in the same direction every time he places it on the right side of the sink. That's where he puts it at precisely 5:58 am every morning. Got the picture?"

"Thanks Ed. See you tomorrow at 11:59 am."

O'Reilly did a search for a night cleaning service on the Internet. He didn't find one. He would pay the $50 charge to use Boncoeur's search engine this time. Normally, he'd scout for a night cleaner on the Net himself. Tonight he didn't feel like it. Boncueur's service would take care of all the details for him after he typed the question on the computer, "Can you find a night cleaning service, have them clean O'Reilly & Associates office, and confirm the office has been cleaned?"

After O'Reilly typed in his credit card number, "Yes" was the response. If he could only get his twelve associates to tidy up their desks as easily. He didn't take the risk. He gave another $50 to www.request&confirm.com. Each of his associates would get a Boncoeur Computer Generated Auditory Batman signal in their email tomorrow morning. He typed in the message. "Important business. Must bring tie. Must bring white shirt with collar. No holes. No jeans. No t-shirts. T-shirt underneath white collar shirt is OK if the shirt doesn't have any logos. Except O'Reilly Associate company t-shirt. Allright to wear that one. You still have to wear the white collar shirt overneath it. You must clean desk by 9am."

Someone pounded on the door. The sound originated below the doorknob. John's little girl opened the door. He took his mind off business.

"Daddy will you tuck me in?"

"Sure thing, sugarplum." Must be his daughter's bedtime. He yawned. He checked the clock on the study wall. Where had the evening gone? The time was 8pm. "Are you sure you want me to tuck you in now? Bedtime isn't for another half hour."

Kathy nodded her head as she yawned. She reached for her Father's hand. "Daddy can I divorce you like Mommy can?"

John eye's opened. He picked up his daughter, holding her in his arms, his face to hers. He smiled. "If you ever tried to divorce me, I would hire the best lawyer in all of Missouri to keep you from doing so. You know who that lawyer would be?"

Kathy yawned. She shook her head.

"Your mother. I'd hire her. She would never ever let you divorce me."

Kathy giggled. She didn't completely understand what Daddy meant, but she could tell from Daddy's voice inflection, Daddy had made a funny, a very good one.

Her Father carried his little girl to her bedroom adjacent the master bedroom. His thoughts of a message on the sign in front of Hope Montessori lit up in his mind like the marquee on the Fox, St. Louis's grandest theatre, where he saw a show last week with his wife.

The words on the marquee read, "All children are gifted. Some wait to open their packages later than others." The gift his daughter's best friend would ask of her parents this Christmas cost nothing. Yet no monetary promotion in the world granted to O'Reilly's next door neighbor would compare to the priceless request Katy would ask of Santa this year.

How was he going to explain to Kathy next week why her best friend didn't like the gift Kathy gave to her at Hope Montessori's gift exchange next week?

CHAPTER 21

...not having enough fun.

John cocked his head back to see if he could see the top of the Mercantile Building, one of the tallest of skyscrapers in downtown St. Louis. He couldn't. The letters atop the edifice, Mercantile, visible from Interstate 40, were no where to be seen. Nor could he see any movement of the inhabitants within. The structure, composed of dark paned glass, did not permit the interior to be exposed. Built on a foundation of concrete many feet deeper than the sidewalk next the building entrance he stood upon, the building did not sway in the slightest in the impending September squall. He held onto his Cardinal baseball hat on a windy late afternoon with one hand. Blown by a howling gust, he missed the entrance to the door with the other, instead, touching a piece of the building's framework, a cold steel beam adjacent the Mercantile Building's entrance.

The blunt stillness of the air upon exiting the outdoor wind was deafening. His sneakers made no noise on the marble floor. No other footsteps could be heard in the Mercantile Building lobby. At 4pm no one was on the ground floor. Only a row of large ceramic bowls greeted the newcomer. Each bowl, containing a tall artificial plant, stood silently in the lobby. Each bowl's plant soldier guarded an adjacent glass door encased between two columns of steel. John opened the door to let some sound in. He wondered why the doors were capable of opening or closing in either direction. The steel beams felt much colder on the inside than on the outside. John tried to get his arms around the fake plant containers. He thought about trying to pick one up. If only his arms were a few inches longer.

He looked at the long row of elevators, more than twenty, each directly opposite an entrance twenty feet away. Beside each elevator was a sequence of numbers. Too many numbers beside too many elevators produced agitation in his stomach as his eyes strained to cipher the information on the wall. The old man hadn't told him what floor Thompson & Coburn was located. John's fear subsided when he saw the directory listing. Thompson & Coburn was located on the 33rd floor. He hit the up button on the elevator next to the numbers 1-40. A minute later the elevator door opened, closed, and nudged upwards with a lone passenger.

John tried to remember the last time he'd been in an elevator. He couldn't. He couldn't recall the date, but he was definitely going up in this one. He recollected his visit to the doctor two weeks ago.

The doctor asked two questions. "Any changes in appetite or sleep?"

"No."

"Any changes in mood?"

He told the doctor he had made a friend. He told the doctor he was feeling a little better and though he hadn't completed reading all of Upgrading and Repairing Pcs he had nearly finished another book, Computer Networking for Dummies. The doctor handed him a prescription for Prozac. Same dosage.

John recalled a few visits he had made with the old man. Though the old man was busy with writing his new book, he listened to John more than the doctor did. The old man wanted to know if he had taken a look at the magazine.

"No."

"Well, come back when you get around to takin' a look at her."

John opened the magazine but he only got as far as looking at the jokes on the flip side of the centerfold. He enjoyed the joke about the Irish man drinking three beers to remember his Brothers back in Ireland. He told Don he looked at the magazine and liked the joke. He asked the old man the next day why the joke was circled.

"Glad ya liked it, kid. That one a classic. What da ya think of the naked lady. I dated her ya know. She pretty hot, ya?"

"I guess." John didn't know. He hadn't looked.

Don went on to say after giving a detailed analysis of her bodily attributes, " If you can't dream what's the point in living? Dreamin' don't cost a cent unless ya dream ya life away. Try this one. Maybe a Miss September more you style. What da ya think of her long black hair?"

The old man opened up the magazine in front of the boy. "Now her hair coverin' her boobies so it all right to take a peek."

And John looked. And he looked some more. And he looked not only at the long flowing waves of hair concealing her breasts but also the hair covering her body elsewhere. He stared at one place in particular until the old man handed him the magazine.

"An' don't worry about messin' her up, I got five more just like her. Let me hear the line a gave ya to say to the lawyer."

"I don't have time for a lot of fun."

"Nope. Ya got ta say it just like I told ya. Say it exactly like this, 'I don't have time for a lot of fun.'"

The extent of their conversations from this point on for a solid week was the exact pronunciation of the sentence "I don't have time for a lot of fun." Each word was practiced one at a time. All nuances to the minutest detail were choreographed repeatedly.

"Start with a facial expression full of sadness, then a dash of snarl, simmer with a trace of a smile, and then get ready to poke your toothpick to check ya cooked the cake all the way."

"I don't have time for a lot of fun."

"You got the first part down pat, kid. Now you've got to smile at the end. Try lifting your eyebrows. That'll might do in place of a smile but ya gonna have to say the word, 'fun', with a lot more fun."

John opened the September '77 issue of Playboy every night. He read the article about the up and coming next revolution in computing repeatedly. The article had predicted by the year 2000 everyone would own a personal computer. John found this forecast fascinating. Again he read the jokes. He liked the one about the elderly man and the lady with panty hose. The old man wouldn't say why this one was circled either.

Don replied, "As long as you can dream, life is good. Go back an' take 'nother look the picture of her unbuttoning her white blouse and slippin' off her black skirt. That'll get ya pumped for sure. I really like those black high heels of hers. I should. I bought 'em for her."

The number 29 flashed above the elevator door. John remembered the date. Today was Tuesday, September 29th. He had requested today off from both jobs. He hadn't taken a day off in over six months except Sunday. He was glad he did. For a week prior to today he looked forward to having the day off. Today he would be doing something different. He dreamed, as best he could, about what his one day vacation would be like and why the old man wanted him to say the sentence about not having time for fun.

This was his dream surrounding the sentence. He was going to see a lawyer. He received a speeding ticket nine months ago for doing 40 mph in a 35. He told the officer he was late for work. Nevertheless, speeding was speeding. The policeman gave him a citation. He couldn't take the time off from work to go to driver's school to get the points taken off his driving record. As a result, his car insurance increased from $1250 to $1400 year. Maybe the lawyer could help him get a better insurance rate. If the lawyer could save him some money, he could afford the subscription to Computer Shopper he always wanted. That would be fun. This was the extent of his dream until he extended his creativeness by imaging the lawyer's office already had a subscription to Computer Shopper with twelve issues in the lobby ready to be thrown away. He could use a free subscription to Computer Shopper if no one else wanted the periodicals.

John's dream ended when the elevator door's opened to a crowded lobby of the law firm, Thompson & Coburn. With fortune 100 businesses as clients and an hourly service rate of a hundred dollars every fifteen minutes billed only in hourly increments, Donald Murphy's retainer served only as an entrance fee to sit in the lobby. John enjoyed his plush chair with fancy woodwork on the arms much more than the reading material. He leafed through an issue of Forbes, a magazine not nearly as entertaining as Computer Shopper.

The carpet was plush green, the same color as the grass at the fishing hole. The walls were a hue of blue the same color as a cloudless sky at the lake. Bordering the edge of wall at the ceiling was a strip of wallpaper with flying birds. John dreamed of taking a nap here. He couldn't. The chair didn't sit correctly for sleeping.

He was five minutes early for his appointment with the lawyer. John had asked the old man what he was suppose to do when he arrived at the law office.

The old man hurriedly replied, "Just tell Kelly the receptionist I sent ya. She take care of ya. She cute, too." Don described Kelly in detail, ending with "Think about her when ya lookin' at Miss September."

Kelly wasn't the receptionist today. This receptionist told John she was a temporary from Manpower Temporary Workforce filling in for Kelly who took the day off as a vacation day. John looked briefly at the new receptionist. She was about his age. From his sitting position John could tell she was having problems operating the computer at her desk. Her mouse scurried about the mouse pad in complete chaos. John dreamed about getting out of his seat and assisting her with her computer problem. He didn't make his dream a reality. He couldn't with his perception of his self.

A minute later John overheard a conversation between her and another office girl filing folders in a room behind the receptionist desk.

"He says he's here because a Mr. Murphy asked him to come for a 4 pm appointment but he doesn't know the lawyer's name he's suppose to see. Can you help me look up Mr. Murphy's lawyer?"

"I remember Mr. Murphy." There was a moment of silence. "Don't bother with the appointment book. The computer is having a bad screen saver day. His lawyer was." More moments of silence. "Started with S. It's Stein. Mr. Murphy's lawyer is Stein."

John and the temp walked down the hallway. John's head pointed at the carpet below. He followed his guide's feet before him. He passed leather shoes. He passed sneakers. His guide stopped. He looked ahead. In front of him was a pair of black heels exactly like the ones Miss September wore except shorter. He looked up, but not at the heel's occupant. He opted to read the sign on the wall adjacent the office the heels were located. The office of Miss Lilleth Steinem, J.S.D. was not John O'Reilly's final destination. His escort guided him to the office of Mr. Howard Stern across the hallway.

"Please have a seat Mr. Murphy. Mr. Stein will be with you shortly." She smiled at John. "You're suppose to look at your watch because I'm suppose to start billing Mr. Murphy's session now."

John looked at his watch and nodded his head.

"Would you like a cup of coffee or a refreshment?"

John declined.

When the temporary receptionist closed the Mr. Stein's office door John jogged over to window. With his Cardinal hat in his hand he peered out the 31st floor observation deck to catch a bird's eye view of the interior of Busch Stadium. This was the first time he'd ever seen inside the home of the St. Louis Cardinals except on TV. He didn't want Mr. Stein to find him in a comprising position behind the lawyer's desk, a position he knew to be out of fair play. A few seconds passed before his mind could make his feet move. When he sat down he was winded. He had sprinted to his chair, steeling home plate safely, without being caught.

The door opened. Mr. Stein walked right by him without any indication of another in his office. John looked at the man. He was large, extremely large at the hips and waist. The last few buttons on the bottom of his white shirt with a ketchup stain and a yellow collar were held but by a single thread. With each step he took, the cloth of his shirt strained to support the roll of fat shaking underneath. His armpits were soaked with sweat. The seat of his pants was soaked also, all the way down the back of his pant legs to his knee. A rear view of Mr. Stein's head revealed he was bald, even though Mr. Stein had skillfully swung a slice of long hair from the part adjacent his ear to cover his bald spot. As Mr. Stein lugged his body into his extra wide seat with a docking procedure akin to removing a boat from water, John noticed from a front view, Mr. Stein appeared to have a full head of hair. Mr. Stein looked at the huge pile of paper scattered over his desk in no discernable pattern. One thought went through John's mind. How was a fat man with a messy desk going to help him have fun?

Mr. Stein peered over his paper mess. "Who are you?"

The boy shook. "I'm John O'Reilly. Mr. Murphy sent me."

Mechanically, Mr. Stein looked at his wall clock. "The time is now 4:21. Four o'clock? I don't have an appointment with any Murphy or anyone. Get out of here! I'm busy."

John apologized and closed Mr. Stein's office quietly. Miss Steinum was standing next to her desk with her back to John's stuck eyes. She was tall with long flowing legs concealed behind black pantyhose. Her skirt was black, slightly longer than knee length. Her heels gave her one-inch of additional height bringing her height to six feet. John opened the five fingers of his hand as he extended his arm. Miss Steinum was several feet away but his eyes believed his hand was touching her butt. She looked exactly like Miss September except her white blouse was tucked in her skirt, her sleeves were not rolled up, and her black hair was not free flowing but rather pinned in a tight little ball. He told himself to stop dreaming. He found the temporary receptionist at her desk reading Cosmopolitan magazine.

"Excuse me." John waited a few seconds for head to turn. "Mr. Stein told me he doesn't have an appointment with Mr. Murphy or anyone."

The mouse on the mouse pad started spinning in circles. "This stupid computer doesn't do anything. I've never seen a more dull screen saver than this all black one."

As she exercised her hand muscles, John inspected her computer. The computer wasn't turned on. With the flick of a switch, John let there be light upon the dark screen.

"What's that?" The receptionist pointed at the screen as she smiled in awe at John, the temporary's computer god who happened to show just at the right moment.

"That's Windows 98 starting."

She smiled. She put one hand on the desk closer to John's body hovering over the computer monitor John's cheek muscles flicked hesitantly. He tried lifting his eyebrows. The pipsqueak couldn't. Her hand went back to the mouse.

"I know how to work the appointment manager program but I don't know to start it."

John pointed at the screen and asked her to double click on icon labeled 'Appointment manager.' She asked John to do it for her. As he did so he noticed the article in Cosmo the receptionist was reading was titled, "Fifty ways to meet your boyfriend in the office." He started the program noting the appointment book was an Access 95 database application. She thanked him.

Then she said, "You're smart."

John thanked her but said he hadn't done much. He didn't talk more than thanking her. He couldn't. He couldn't think of anything to say.

She operated the computer program. "Miss Steinum is Mr. Murphy's lawyer."

Again John and the temp walked down the hallway. John's dream of a Computer Shopper subscription disappeared to a dream of holding the receptionist's hand down the hallway permanently. She was pretty. He liked the way she swung her hips as she walked down the hallway beside him.

"Miss Steinum."

Lileth looked up from her tidy and organized desk. Behind the desk was a bookcase full of law books, each carefully aligned row after row after row. She stood up to greet her next client.

"This is Mr. Murphy. He has a four o'clock appointment."

John looked at the receptionist, "Uh. My name is John."

"This is John. He has a four o'clock appointment with you, Miss Steinum."

"Thank you, receptioinst."

"Hello, John. I am Miss Lileth Steinum; however, I prefer to waive the formalities as you. You may call me Lileth. Please have a seat."

Miss Steinum closed her office door. John sat in a chair across the desk from her thinking a single thought, the thought of the pretty receptionist whose name he did not know. The receptionist sulked down the hall with only the thought of being a no name receptionist.

"Please accept my apology on behalf of Thompson & Coburn concerning the error regarding the confusion resulting from the improper presentation of the selected lawyer chosen by Mr. Murphy to counsel the said client on his estate management situation."

John didn't understand anything Lileth said beyond the first nine words. The drawerless desk of solid oak with four ornately etched legs provided an open view beneath the table top. She crossed her legs in full view of John. Her pantyhose concealed the skin of her legs. John looked at the pure white skin of Lileth's hand, the only flesh of her body exposed bedside her face. Though her skin was soft, veins protruded and tendons flexed skin no longer taut. John looked at her alabaster skin with no make up applied on her face. She had small wrinkles on her forehead and several smile lines. The skin on her jaw sagged. She was not as pretty as the receptionist who was twenty years younger and brought home a yearly income ten times less than the lawyer before him with a $200,000 a year salary.

"I accept." John had no idea what apology he accepted.

"I would have acted sooner to prevent the error which did indeed occur; however, as Mr. Stein and I do not have a suitable working relationship I chose to refrain from intervening the said misrepresentation thus by avoiding a possible conflict with the said lawyer."

John nodded his head.

"I loathe Mr. Stein. Mr. Stein is disgusting." She snarled. "Men." She smiled at the boy. "Would you mind if I present myself in a less formal fashion."

"I guess not."

Lileth undid a clip in her hair to allow her shiny black hair to unfold. She waved her head from side to side before the boy. He gazed upon her wavy hair resting upon her slender bosom. In so doing, she removed twenty years of age from the boy's eyes. Directly across the desk from him, according to his eyes, sat Miss September.

"I recently received a permanent. Do you like my hair?"

John nodded his head. He could have done so permanently. Only when she continued to speak did his head cease to throb up and done. His tenseness in the chair eased.

"Good. Let us begin to conduct our scheduled meeting. Note the time is now 4:49. As dictated by the prearranged conduct of fees for services agreement arranged prior to this meeting between the law firm of Thompson & Coburn, henceforth referred to as the firm, and Mr. Murphy, henceforth referred to as the client, a fee for a conduct of one hour of services rendered will be issued. This statement is not implied to infer the receipt of a bill for said services has been issued nor does said services rendered construe a bill as pursuant to the statues of the State of Missouri pertaining to fees rendered upon services issued. Cross verification with a third party observant to said time of start of said scheduled meeting between the firm and the client will be conducted. Do you accept this verbal agreement?"

"Ya."

Lileth removed one book from the bookcase. John watched her stretch to reach for the top shelf and then bend at the hips to find the book she was in search of on the bottom shelf. John quickly searched inside his pocket as he pretended to adjust his seat. He read the title on the cover, "Problems and Materials on Decedents' Estates and Trusts", as she placed the book on the desk.

"Good. Let us begin. Mr. Murphy, henceforth referred to as the settlor, has selected me to counsel said settlor on matters pertaining to Estate and Foreclosure Law."

John just looked.

"This means I'm his Executor Attorney."

John nodded his head to confirm he understood her. He wanted to say something. What had the old man told him to say to her? He couldn't remember. He strained to think of something to say. Something sounding smart.

"Has Mr. Murphy made a lot of money?"

"We are currently assaying the settlor's numerous financial holdings. Presently, assets in excess of $50 million have been accounted; however, the settlor also has a multitude of outstanding debts substantially detracting from the settlor's estate value. For example, Mr. Murphy has invested considerable capitol in land on the Cayman Islands which is in dispute with hundreds of other claims who may or may not have privileged defacto ownership to the land in contention with Mr. Murphy's claim."

John just nodded his head.

"This means Mr. Murphy has bought shantytown on Grand Cayman Island, and as he has not added value to the land in the form of any home or building otherwise, the inhabitants, or squatters, may have rightful ownership of the land."

"Mr. Murphy says he built a house there."

"His title to the land is currently being evaluated; however, the possibility of the outcome being positive for the settlor appears unlikely as the surveying team is unable to distinguish Mr. Murphy's possible habitat from any other dweller's inhabitation as each dwelling shares a common wall with another dwelling. Serves him right."

She hissed. "Do you know Mr. Murphy has been married in excess of ten times? With at least three other possible marital relationships in contention? Men." Her tongue flickered. "Simply disgusting. Mr. Murphy did not even have the decency to prepare a prenuptial agreement with any of his former spouses thus making my burden of obtaining for the settlor no entitlement of any prior financial accumulation to any former spouse upon verification of settlor's post mortum deceasing ceasing all claims to a one year allowance following Mr. Murphy's deceasement."

John had not a clue to the lawyer's wording. He was trying to remember what the old man had told him to tell the lawyer so he could have some fun. He shook his head in an up and down fashion.

Lileth looked into her law book. Her fingers sifted through the pages. She was searching for a particular piece of information. She spoke softly. "Have you ever been married?"

"No." John strained to recall what to say to have fun.

"Neither have I." She smiled at John. "I should not talk about my clients in such a manner. I too have had problems." Lileth dug her face into the book on her desk. "I am not a licensed financial planner." She softly pouted, "I should have become one instead of spending twelve years in higher education including Harvard Law School. I did not have time for any fun in my twenties."

John nodded. His brain uncontrollably searched for the sentence Mr. Murphy had told him to say to the lawyer.

"Mr. Murphy has selected you, John. John, tell me what is your last name?"

"O'Reilly." John understood this question. His answer slowed his mind. He looked at the book on the desk. He had a problem, too. He could only remember the first two words of the sentence Mr. Murphy told him to say.

Lileth spread open the book to the leaves with a soft fold at the edge. "John O'Reilly you are Mr. Murphy's selected primary beneficiary as stipulated by the Revised statues of Missouri Law Section 419.020. In this state, Mr. John O'Reilly, you, who shall constantly have in good order, and of the like, shall not be liable nor conspicuously suspended any such articles aforesaid."

Lileth ran her middle finger gently down the crease between the leaves with a gently fold.

"Anything to the contrary notwithstanding shall voluntary comply without loss thereof or damage thereto unless the same has actually delivered by such to said beneficiary or the beneficiary authorized agent. Do you accept this agreement properly referred to as an Intervivous Trust of free will and without coercion?"

As she completed her last whisper of sensual lawyer verbiage, she spread her legs underneath the table in full view of the boy's wondering eager eyes. Before him was the picture of the beautiful young lady's womanishness previously exposed by Mr. Murphy. He looked at the floor. He recalled the sentence.

Instinctively, without thought, he spoke, "I don't have time for a lot of fun," exactly how the old man told him to say the nine word sentence.

"Neither do I." With one hand she caressed the book. With the other she twirled her hair. She looked at the book. She spoke softly.

"Would you accept an offer to engage in the act of sexual intercourse with me?"

The boy sat in the chair motionless. He thought for a second. Did she say the words "sexual intercourse with someone?"

He looked at her. She returned a congenial smile but he could not reply in turn. He couldn't swallow. He thought about swallowing for a second.

What had the old man told him to do after he said the sentence?

Whatever it was he had to think about swallowing first or he was going to drool on the floor. He felt the first drip of saliva leave his mouth. This was the only part of his body he could feel move in any way. He swallowed. He swallowed deep and long. He gulped a reservoir of accumulated saliva, cooked hot by the oven of his mouth. His mouth was wet enough to wet a whistle. Just whistle. He tried but no tune came out. The old man told him to do something next after he spoke the sentence, something easy to do. He remembered. Count to five.

He started to count in his head. He thought he felt something below his belt throbbing in unison to his numeration, urging him to count faster. With each increment in number he could feel his pelvic region tingle. By the number five, he couldn't take anymore. His blue jeans were ready to bust. He started to tingle all over. He fidgeted in his chair to relieve the tightness in his loins. Ohhhh, the sensation. It occurred to him what he should say now even thought the old man had given him no specific instruction.

"Ya. Oh, yeah,"

Lilleth, the lawyer nearing the onset of menopause smiled warmly. She had been waiting patiently for the boy to give an answer. Now she squirmed in her chair in reply to the boy's body movement. She titled her head a little and shook it slightly from side to side ending with her mouth slightly open and her head cocked back.

The boy interpreted her actions. He knew she was ready to swallow his yearning salivating within his pants into her open reservoir. His legs stiffened following the response from his hidden but now fully elongated sexual leg. His head below his belt beckoned him to expose this leg to the lawyer. His body released from its paralysis. He was ready to spring forth, giving his blossoming manhood to the caress of her red swollen lips. He slid the chair back from the table to do so.

She spoke. "I believe from the actions you have demonstrated thus far our encounter of after hours intercourse will be mutually pleasurable for both parties involved."

John's legs collapsed beneath him. Only the two legs John used for walking purposes. His other member was bent but not incapable of wheeling the boy in his chair to the other side of the desk occupied by the said lawyer. He looked at her pull out several pieces of paper from her briefcase next to the desk.

"First, let us take care of a few formalities."

John's head nodded.

"This is a consent form stipulating I did not at any time conduct the said proposition in any form, manner, or the like which could be construed by the propositionee as harassment of any nature, sexual, of the like or not unlike or any form otherwise. Sign here, please."

John signed. His handwriting wasn't legible. His arm between his legs could have signed his Hancock as well.

"This is a form to be filled by you conducting a survey of your interests, intentions, habits, and any behavioral abnormalities which may prohibit the said intercourse from indeed occurring. Also I will cross reference this survey with my likes and dislikes to guarantee an acceptable compatibility between us did indeed occur."

John's troubled head watched the lawyer finger through the sixty page document.

"Don't worry. I am certain a match has been made. We have something in common. I did not have any fun in my twenties. You have not had any fun in your twenties. We will have fun together. I know we will. Please sign this form verifying you have taken possession of the personality and behavioral abnormality survey with the intention of completing and returning in the pre paid postage envelope by October 15th of this year."

John just gazed.

"If you need an extension to complete the survey I will allow so given the conditions you have stipulated warrant such an extension. You may conduct the survey on audio or videocassette if you prefer. I also have the document digitally stored on floppy diskette. Would you find this medium acceptable? Maybe diskette will be the minimal of all means by which to transport?"

John nodded his head while he doodled his signature. He put the diskette the lawyer had placed in his unopened hand, which she opened for him, into his pant's pocket. He adjusted himself in the process. Though he could no longer do three legged cartwheels he still could not stand without exposing his excitement.

"This is the last form. Please accomplish the tasks outlined in the form as quickly as possible as some time is required until the results can be obtained. Likewise, at any time, you, the propostionee, may feel free to ask of me, the propostioner, of the results of the required tests which I have voluntarily undertaken."

John stared at the form. In bold letters at the top were the words Smith Kline Beechum Medical Laboratory.

"John, this is important. After you provide the hair, mucous, saliva, toenail, fingernail, perspiration, urine, stool, and blood samples you must abstain from any and all forms of sexual activities, blood transfusions, and intravenous drug use for a period of six weeks thereafter which at said time the tests will be duplicated to verify the propositionee is absent of any." She paused. She looked at the boy. "I don't think you have any cooties. But one can never be too safe." She laughed like Mr. Stein next door when he was a chubby fourteen-year old teenager. "Better to be safe than sorry." She laughed again. "I'm not going to ask you for a bone marrow sample. Normally, I do. For you, based on your physical health, I will believe such test can be waived with no risk whatsoever."

John signed his name like he normally would. He completed the paperwork by filling in his address. Once again, he could walk home without embarrassment.

"And please once again on the old man's will."

John signed wondering what power the old man possessed such that by John' will to state one simple sentence a meeting such as this would be produced.

Lileth picked up her briefcase. "This concludes our scheduled meeting. I will contact you concerning our much anticipated encounter via the non electonic mail system."

The minute hand on the wall moved incrementally one notch pointing vertically upward. The clock struck five. It was YaBaDaBa Do time. Though no whistle blew the bedrock upon which the Mercantile Building quaked. The floors vibrated. The walls shook. The doorknob rattled as Lileth locked the door to her office and joined the rest of the herd running for the elevator.

The boy, at her heels, gazed at her stride as he followed her down the hall with not a clue to where he was going. A pair of sneakers stopped him.

"Sir, you dropped your hat," replied a mail clerk about the same age as he.

John picked up his hat.

The elevator labeled I-40 must be the one he needed to stand in line for. This one must be the one going to Interstate Forty. He stood.

"Excuse me, John."

John stared at the pretty receptionist with no name.

"You dropped your hat."

She smiled. He didn't smile back. John didn't say anything. She placed his baseball cap in his hand after she opened his mitt first. John had only one thought on his mind. When he reached home safely he was going to play some ball. He was going to play with himself, pretending to be both the pitcher and the catcher at the same time.

He couldn't find his hat when he opened the door to his apartment. He remembered placing the hat securely on his head as he pushed on the door exiting the lobby. He thought someone in the stampede had said the word, 'bat.' He didn't care. Miss September was waiting for him. He laid the Playboy magazine on his bedroom floor. The catcher took his position as he spread her miniature but true to proportion figure before his crouched stance. He woundup and threw the first pitch. Before he took a swing he noticed a shadow moving on the wall. John, with only his hands in the shape of a cup to shield his equipment from any harm, stood up to close the blinds.

He hoped no one saw. Then he heard a word sounding like 'Herbert.' The voice was definitely feminine. He hoped the voice wasn't of the girl living next door to him who he had met in the hallway. Maybe she said 'Sherbert.' John head tilted toward the floor. From the looks of things he was surely going to go blind.

The End of Episode I

The boy and the old man make friends.

Ryan Austin Clarke

ABOUT THE AUTHOR

Ryan Austin Clarke earned his B.S. in Mathematics and Physics in 1992. For the past nine years he has been a part of the ever-changing world of Information Technology, having held such various positions as field engineer, support analyst, network engineer, database administrator and most recently software developer. In his spare time, to exercise the creative side of his brain, he has written a book of poetry and contributed several articles to the Orlando Sentinel, Central Florida's most significant daily newspaper. He is currently working on a graduate degree in Computer Science. When he's not chained in a cubicle from 9-5, or working on a thesis, he can be found at The Grind, a local coffee shop in St. Louis, Missouri, doing what he enjoys most, writing fiction.